windblowne

windblowne

STEPHEN MESSER

Random House New York

Text copyright © 2010 by Stephen Messer
Jacket art copyright © 2010 by Erwin Madrid

Published in the United States by Random House Children's Books,
a division of Random House, Inc., New York.

Random House and the colophon are registered trademarks
of Random House, Inc.

Visit us on the Web! www.randomhouse.com/kids

Educators and librarians, for a variety of teaching tools,
visit us at www.randomhouse.com/teachers

Library of Congress Cataloging-in-Publication Data
Messer, Stephen, 1972–
Windblowne / by Stephen Messer. — 1st ed.
  p. cm.
Summary: Hapless Oliver, who lives in the trees in the town of
Windblowne, seeks his eccentric great-uncle Gilbert's help in
creating a kite for the all-important kite festival, but when Gilbert
suddenly disappears, Oliver is guided by one of Gilbert's kites in a
quest through different worlds to find him.
ISBN 978-0-375-86195-6 (trade) — ISBN 978-0-375-96195-3
(lib. bdg.) — ISBN 978-0-375-89347-6 (e-book)
[1. Kites—Fiction. 2. Space and time—Fiction. 3. Identity—Fiction.
4. Uncles—Fiction. 5. Fantasy.] I. Title.
PZ7.M554Wi 2010
[Fic]—dc22
2008043777

Printed in the United States of America
10 9 8 7 6 5 4 3 2 1
First Edition

to Miriam

windblowne

1

Oliver sat back on his stool. He was finished. His hands were blistered, his head ached, and his nostrils burned with the stink of boiling glue, but he was sure this one would work. After a lifetime of embarrassments and disappointments that made his toes curl to think about, he'd finally done it. This time he would fly.

For two days Oliver had snipped and sewn, boiled glue in the glue pots, lit new candles when the old ones had burned down to nubs, cursed and sucked on his cuts when he was clumsy with a knife, and paced back and forth crumpling up papers covered with his carefully drawn designs before hurling them into the corners in disgust. Then he would sit at his workbench to draw up new designs, and snip and sew some more. All the while, the midsummer winds had howled ceaselessly outside the treehouse.

Oliver stood, kicking aside discarded fragments of bamboo spars. With a triumphant sweep of his arm, he cleared the workbench. Everything spilled onto the floor with a tumultuous crash. He pulled open drawers and laid out his tools. He had new twine, new reels, his hand-vane, and several other useful odds and ends. He jammed it all into his pack.

He dashed to the window and threw it open. Cold wind blasted into the room. Oliver leaned out into the tossing branches of the oak. He closed his eyes, listening to the winds as they blew over the mountain and through the oaks. They were just right for flying, he decided, but twilight would be settling soon. If he hurried, there would be time for one test flight before the night winds came.

He slammed the window closed, then tore off his smock and hurled it over a stack of rejected spars. He donned his warmest flier's outfit: leather gloves, fur-lined boots, loose-cut pants with toughened knees, a thick sweater, and a heavy wool cap fastened under his chin. Feeling very professional, he slung his pack over his shoulders and, with his creation tucked under one arm, peeked down the hall.

No one had bothered to light the lamps, of course, and the hallway curved into darkness in both directions as it followed the shape of their tree. The only light was a faint flickering spilling through a doorway halfway to the stairs. From within that room came the continuous scratching sound of pen across paper.

Oliver crept down the hall. He had nearly mastered the pattern of the creaky floorboards. *Left two steps, right one step, now over to the wall, then a hop, then left ... no, right!* The floorboard groaned, and Oliver froze as a voice called out.

"Oliver, lad, is that you? Fetch me a cup of tea, will you? There's a lad." As usual, his father's voice sounded distant and distracted.

Oliver peeked into the study. There was the customary sight: his father's back hunched over a desk piled with books and pages covered with cryptic scrawl. The room was nearly dark, as the shades had not been opened and a last flickering candle was about to die. Just beside his father's arm was the untouched cup of tea, now cold, that Oliver had brought up hours ago.

"Yes, Father," Oliver said, trying to hide his creation behind his back on the remote chance his father turned around. "I'll bring it right up."

"There's a lad," his father replied vaguely. His pen had not stopped scratching.

Oliver hurried to the staircase and dashed down into the kitchen. The rest of the treehouse was silent and dark. As he passed the pantry, his stomach growled, and he realized that he had not eaten all day. *No time for that,* thought Oliver. *I'll have a victory dinner when I return.* Yes, a triumphant homecoming involving crowds of people apologizing for all the mockery he'd received over the years. Thinking these happy thoughts, he pushed open the creaking front door.

He stopped on the landing, forty feet up, and looked worriedly at the signs of Windblowne preparing for the coming of night. In the treehouses of nearby oaks, lamps were sputtering to life. Townspeople were reeling in the rope bridges that connected one treehouse to another. On Windswept Way, far below, people were hurrying home, hands thrust deep into pockets and shoulders hunched against the suddenly cold winds.

A brown oak leaf drifted by. Oliver plucked it from

the air. *Another one,* he thought. The leaf was dry and brittle, as though midsummer had been interrupted by autumn. He'd been seeing leaves like this for weeks, and what was most curious was that Oliver, who could normally tell from which of the giant oaks any leaf had fallen, did not recognize these. They had to be from an oak he didn't know, and he was certain he knew almost every oak on the mountain. This meant he was never lost, but from looking at this leaf he could see that the map in his mind must have a gap in it somewhere.

He shook his head. No time to waste on leaves. Oliver yanked his handvane from his pack. He snapped it onto his wrist and held it high. The pointer spun before settling southish. Oliver studied the result with an expert eye. He might not be much good at flying, but he was a superb wind-reader. The north-by-northeast wind was still blowing, best for flying, but the pointer was trembling, indicating an increasingly unsteady flow. The wind's direction and speed would be changing soon. Night was drawing near.

Dare he risk it?

Oliver nodded his head. He did. The kite must be tested tonight.

Down the circular staircase he ran, winding dizzily around the trunk of his familiar home oak, sliding his hand along its bark for luck and comfort. On the ground, he raced across the small front yard. Off to one side was his mother's workshop, and coming from it was the usual cacophonous assortment of muttering, the clash of hammer on chisel, and the occasional loud curse. Surrounding the workshop were several—Oliver was not sure what to call them—perhaps sculptures? that his mother was working on, or had already finished. Oliver could not tell either way. Maybe they had just fallen over. Oliver sighed and kept running.

In a moment he was on Windswept Way, Windblowne's only road, which curled round the mountain from foot to crest like a coiled spring. Oliver ran upward, passing under treehouses high overhead as the winds pushed him higher, faster. He kept furtively to one side of the Way, hoping that the late hour meant he wouldn't be noticed and snickered at. Or worse, prevented from going to the crest at all. He kept running up, up, up as the Way wound higher.

Oliver's fears were realized when he spied a member of the Windblowne Watch waddling down the Way and lighting the oil lamps on either side. Like all members of the Watch, he was fat and friendly and long retired from a life of flying. Normally the Watch had little to do in peaceful Windblowne, but each midsummer they were forced to rise from their usual seats on the balcony of their tavern headquarters to manage the crowds of tourists who came for the Festival.

Oliver put the kite behind his back and slowed to what he hoped was an inconspicuous stroll.

"Oh! Hullo, Oliver!" the Watchman said cheerily as he lit the next lamp.

"Hullo," said Oliver quickly, edging past.

"I say," said the Watchman in surprise. "That's not a kite you have there, is it?"

"No," said Oliver.

"Oh," replied the Watchman, looking puzzled. "Well, that's good. The night winds are coming, you know. No time to be flying!" He pulled a sheet of stiff paper from within his coat and affixed it to the lamppost.

Oliver resumed his dash for the crest the moment the Watchman's back was turned.

Oliver had been trying to ignore those papers, but it wasn't easy. They lined the Way every midsummer, tacked to trees and fences and lampposts and the occasional wagon. They littered the lands beyond the mountain too, their message carried far and wide by the winds. Some of them blew across his path, mocking him, and he kicked at them savagely. He knew their message by heart:

YE OLDE FESTIVAL OF
KITES
IN ITS 455TH YEAR

———

THE MOUNTAIN TOWNE OF
WINDBLOWNE INVITES
ONE AND ALL

———

COMMENCING ON THE NINTH
DAY OF THE SECOND MOON

———

FIVE DAYS OF FANTASTIC
CREATIONS AND DARING
FEATS

———

THE WONDER OF ALL THE WORLD

———

The Legendary Fliers of Windblowne and the Tournament of Champions!

Today was the Fifth Day of the Second Moon. Four days remained.

The wind blowing down from the crest brought a chorus of young voices, shouts mixed with laughter. Oliver grimaced. The voices belonged to those he had most been hoping to avoid, but there was no help for it. He marched grimly upward, gripping his kite.

A group of children came into view, all carrying kites. Oliver felt his usual shudder of envy, and a surge of embarrassment for his own kite. For his classmates' kites were more than just kites; they were brilliantly painted eagles, bats, and dragons. The elaborate kites had hinges and latches that allowed them to be folded flat and carried, and then opened to full size when launched. These were kites that were, without question, worthy of the Festival, and all of the children were brimming with excitement and confidence.

They spotted Oliver. He braced himself.

"Marcus, do you see that?" one of them called, in

mock astonishment. "Oliver has gotten hold of another kite somehow!"

Marcus held his eagle kite behind his back as though shielding it. "Oh, Oliver," he said, shaking his head sadly. "What did that poor, defenseless thing do to deserve this fate?" He turned to his friend. "Alain, do you think there's room in the trees for another one of Oliver's kites?"

Alain looked thoughtful. "I'm not sure," he said. "They're getting pretty crowded up there. It might be more merciful just to burn this one. Need a match, Oliver?"

Peals of jeering laughter were carried off on the wind as Oliver quickened his pace, leaving the others behind.

All but one. A black-haired girl with a dragon kite broke away and hurried after Oliver. She had a red knit pouch slung over one shoulder, and it bounced on her hip as she ran. He groaned. Of all the humiliating episodes in his ill-fated flying career, this girl represented one of the worst. She had spent months making one of the most beautiful kites Windblowne had ever seen, a school of flying fish fashioned from silk and bamboo. In a moment of poor judgment, she had asked Oliver if he would like to fly it. Unable to resist, he had accepted the reels—and to his horror, had promptly steered the kite directly into the ground, destroying it. The violence with which he had managed to accomplish this was a frequent topic of discussion at school.

"Ilia!" Alain shouted from down the Way. "Better stay away from Oliver! Bad luck before the Festival."

Ilia ignored him and dashed up beside Oliver. "Oliver," she said anxiously, "you're not going to the crest, are you?"

He did not answer. He wished she would stop being so nice about everything. She ought to hate him for what he had done.

"Well," said Ilia after an awkward pause. "Be careful, Oliver. The night winds are coming."

"Ilia!" shouted several of the others.

"Wait!" she called. She rummaged in her red knit pouch and produced a tiny golden kite charm on which a name had been etched—*Ilia*. She offered it to Oliver. "For luck. You can give it back to me tomorrow."

Oliver shook his head, wounded. Why did Ilia think he needed her luck? "No thanks."

"Well, good luck anyway," said Ilia. Before Oliver

could react, she pressed the charm into his hand, then raced down the mountain to her friends.

Well, that's over with, thought Oliver miserably, dropping the charm into his pocket. But then he heard more voices, carried on the wind—more classmates, coming home late from practice. More ridicule. He would have turned around if he weren't so desperate.

He paused. How desperate? Desperate enough to use his secret path? It lay just ahead. . . .

No, he reminded himself sternly. *That's only for emergencies. Someone might see!*

But the voices were advancing, and the pointer on his handvane was wobbling violently. If anything qualified as an emergency, this was it.

He spied the entrance to the path, hidden behind a seemingly impenetrable wall of brush. He would never have discovered it were it not for two oaks located on either side, like twin sentinels guarding the trail, their lower branches dipping down just so.

Here lies the path, the sentinels seemed to say.

The voices were nearly upon him. He dove into the wall of brush, gliding through an almost invisible gap. From the safety of this hiding place he watched as more children passed, laughing and waving their wonderful kites. He burned at the sight. He burned particularly because he wanted to join them so very badly. When the children were gone, he turned and stumbled up the path.

Although it was a more direct route to the crest than Windswept Way, the path was overgrown and difficult to traverse. Fallen tree limbs mostly concealed what remained of the trail. Oliver crashed along. It must have been years since anyone had walked this old path regularly. He had used it only a few times himself.

A flash of color caught his eye.

Oliver crouched beside a sharp bit of broken oak limb. Hanging from the tip of it was the tiniest scrap of crimson silk. He touched it.

Kite silk.

Someone else had come this way.

Oliver stood, furious. This path was *his* secret! Now that he looked, he could see other signs—snapped twigs, footprints. Someone else had been through. Not far along he found a low branch that had a torn bit of wool on it, like the wool from which his own flying cap was made.

Oliver began to smash along. Maybe the person was

still on the trail. Maybe he could catch up. Perhaps the other person would be willing to keep the secret. It would be better than having all of Windblowne tramping up and down the path every day. . . .

But whoever it was had not gone to the crest. The trail of snapped twigs and footprints and torn thread ended abruptly, halfway up. Or rather, it didn't end but turned off the path and went deeper into the forest.

A cascade of dead leaves tumbled past.

Odd! Oliver thought, and for a moment he wavered. Then determination returned as he saw how the twilight gloom was gathering. He hurried up the path, resolving to come back after the Festival and explore this mystery further.

Soon he neared the crest.

As always, Oliver thrilled to the sound of the rising, rushing winds racing through the oaks. Normally he liked to look up into their tossing branches. Not tonight, though. Tonight he kept his eyes fixed firmly on the path. *No more distractions, Oliver,* he told himself. *Focus.*

He emerged onto the crest through another invisible gap in the brush. The oakline ended abruptly at the crest border, forming a wide circle around it. From this line the open ground rose a quarter mile to the peak, where the most unpredictable and treacherous winds blew. Nothing was able to grow on the crest itself but a thin covering of hardy mountain grass. Strong as they were, even the giant oaks could not withstand the crest winds.

He had hoped he would be the only one here at this late hour. Surely no one, at least no one who wasn't as desperate as Oliver, would risk damaging his kite or himself this close to the Festival. But near the peak, a few daring fliers were getting in some final minutes of practice. Oliver recognized them. They were all young men and women who had nearly made the final rounds last summer. They were braving the winds in these last hours, hoping to find some edge that could catapult them to the championship this year.

As he removed reels and twine from his pack, Oliver could not resist an intense and grudging admiration for those fliers. They were handling, with expert skill, the most sophisticated type of power kite, built specifically for jumping. Each kite had precision folds and angles designed to master the shifting winds of the crest. Complicated lines wound down from the kites to the reels held by the fliers, who heaved on the multiple strands, causing the kites to plunge in breathtaking dives and rise in swooping arcs. The kites danced about in complex forms, sometimes joining their neighbors to create intricate aerial patterns. Each kite commanded the air, seeming as though at any moment it might break free and fly off on its own, sweeping all of the others from the sky.

As Oliver watched, a flier left the group and fought toward the peak. Oliver held his breath.

For the briefest moment, the flier balanced herself, pulling hard against the unpredictable gusts, jousting with the wind. Then, in one expert motion, she swung her kite into the teeth of the gale and jumped.

She flew up and out, over the heads of her friends, who whooped and cheered. She twisted in flight, still in control, her legs kicking. At last she landed, far from the peak. Oliver was in awe. Her leap was just yards shy of the flat granite marker that noted the spot of the farthest jump on record. The dream of every flier in town was to break that record, but the marker had not been moved in almost fifty years. For this jumper, however, the extra practice was paying off. She looked as though she were ready to enter the first rank and threaten that mark.

With a guilty start, Oliver realized that he had gotten

so caught up in watching that flier that he had delayed longer than he intended. He checked his handvane. The pointer was dancing wildly. He knew he ought to come back in the morning. The other fliers were urgently reeling in their kites.

There's still time for a quick test, he decided. He looked nervously at his kite. It was a simple flat-wing model, or at least an attempt at one. He had heated the spine too quickly, and the whole thing was rather bent. He tried to ignore the other flaws, the clumsy rips and awkward joins. "You're not so bad," he whispered, stroking the kite in an attempt to smooth out its wrinkled sails. "I'll just give you one test flight and then fix you up in time for the Festival."

He looked around sheepishly, glad that no one was nearby to hear him talking to one of his kites, a childish habit that he could not seem to break.

He made his final preparations hastily, fastening lines to each side of the kite and securing them to the reel. He gripped the reel firmly in his hard leather glove. Time to fly. He grasped the kite with his other hand and, with what he hoped was a smooth, correct motion, tossed it up to catch the winds.

And then he heard it—an oncoming roar. The oaks behind him signaled their warning with a furious flailing: *The night winds have come!*

Oliver's kite was torn to shreds instantly. He was thrown to the ground, his breath knocked from him. He grabbed desperately for his things, but they were whipped away—his pack, his handvane torn from his wrist, all gone. Oliver crawled back to the safety of the oaks as broken branches smashed into the ground around him, leaves and dirt stung his face, and winds screamed in his ears. He reached the trunk of the nearest oak and struggled to his feet. He leaned, heart pounding, his chest thick with fear. He could have been killed.

Numbly, Oliver staggered back through the oaks to his hidden trail. Everything was gone. All of his equipment. His hope of entering the Festival. His kite. Everything.

And when he put his hand into his pocket, he discovered that he had lost Ilia's golden kite charm, too.

He stumbled brokenly down the mountain, fighting tears, hardly hearing the din raised by the oaks as the night winds battered and raged. On another night he would have listened in rapture, but tonight the sounds seemed full of despair.

Oliver had lost his lamp along with his pack, and he might have wandered in complete darkness if his way were not lit by the two moons, which traveled together through the night sky every midsummer. Nahfa, the larger, and Aspin, his smaller companion, signaled the start of the Festival when they drew near each other in the sky. Normally he would have stopped and gazed at them shining together, but tonight they only reminded him that he would be watching the Festival from the sidelines again this year, as he probably would every year for the rest of his life.

Consumed with dark thoughts, he plodded down, shoving branches aside. In his misery and fatigue, he did not notice the slim form that slipped from the shadows, wearing a heavy wool cap fastened under its chin, watching him intently as he disappeared down the secret path, toward Windswept Way and home.

2

When Oliver woke, his bedroom was still dark. Normally he left his heavy curtains open so that the morning sunlight would wake him. Last night he had left them closed, and now his room was cheerless and dim. He sat up, blinking, wondering how late it was. It had been nearly sunrise when he had finally gone to bed.

He had spent hours eliminating everything from his room that reminded him of his failures. Gone from the walls were the paintings of kites. The racks for kite-smithing supplies were bare, and the chest that normally held reels and twine stood empty. Nothing lay on the workbench except a book titled *Careers in Mining,* which sat open to page one. Last night, he had resolved to stay up and read as much of it as he possibly could. Today, he resolved to read page two.

Even his not-so-secret drawer had been yanked open and emptied. He had tried to build it in the side of his workbench, as a place to hold his most treasured possessions, but since he was as skilled in carpentry as he was in kitesmithing, the drawer was crude and obvious and terribly unsecret. Anyway, it had held only kite supplies, and was empty now, so he didn't care if it was secret or not.

He dressed slowly. With no kite, he had no reason to wear his flying clothes, and so he dressed only in a simple tunic, jacket, and trousers. In his closet he found his fur-lined boots, which he promptly kicked under the bed, where they joined the rest of his crumpled flying outfit. He peered around the room for something else to kick, but there wasn't much left. He wondered if a tourist had come across the bundle of kiting gear lying beside the Way. Maybe they'd be able to make something useful out of Oliver's things. Oliver certainly hadn't.

Downstairs, his parents were sitting at the breakfast table. His mother was wearing her dusty smock and wolfing down cold meat and berry juice while waving her knife in the air and talking to his father. Oliver saw that no fire had been made in the stove, so he began to build one.

"This sculpture will be the best yet in the Anguish series," his mother said excitedly, stabbing the air with her fork. "It represents my finest achievement in anguish!"

"Yes, dear," his father said remotely, in much the same tone as he had asked Oliver for tea. His pen did not hesitate as it flew across the pages. He was still dressed in his nightclothes and had nothing before him but his papers and an untouched glass of juice.

"I mean it," she continued. "We've got tourists coming from all over for that *thing*. The Festival, I mean. Some of them will be the sort who can appreciate art, unlike that fool mayor!"

"Yes, dear."

"When they see *Anguish Number Seven* out there projecting despair, they'll forget all about those frivolous kites and start focusing on the world around them! There's another leaf death in progress, just like six years ago. Something must be done!" She thumped the table. Dust rose from her smock and hung, undecided, in the air.

"Yes, dear." The pen scratched away.

They continued in this fashion as Oliver coaxed the

fire to life. He wondered if his mother would be having this conversation with thin air if he and his father walked out of the room, and decided that she probably would. When the flames were leaping in the stove, Oliver began to fry bacon. The smell filled the kitchen.

His father sniffed and raised his head, his pen finally stopping. "Say, that smells good. Hullo, Oliver!"

"Good morning," Oliver replied, concentrating on his bacon. He added eggs to the skillet, and more bacon for his father.

His mother gulped down her juice and stood abruptly, yanking on a hat. "Yes, good morning, dear. If anyone needs anything, I'll be busy in my workshop! No time to dawdle!" She grabbed Oliver and gave him a fierce kiss on the top of his head; then out the door she went. Oliver knew she wouldn't be back until dark.

His father was looking around the kitchen as though seeing it for the first time. "Ah yes, the Festival," he said. "I suppose it is about that time, isn't it? I'd forgotten!"

Oliver brought their breakfasts to the table and began to eat.

His father's wandering gaze settled on Oliver. "So," he said. "Are you flying a kite in the Festival, lad?"

Surprised, Oliver paused with a forkful of food halfway to his mouth. He shook his head.

"Why not?" said his father. "You like kites, don't you?"

Oliver hardly knew what to say. He had not thought it possible, but his father had reached a new low point in his sad history of oblivion. Oliver waited for him to go back to his writing. But the man kept staring at him, a vaguely puzzled expression on his face. He had actually put down his pen, although his hand was still resting on it. It occurred to Oliver that his father must be waiting for an answer, so he said, "I don't have a kite." Oliver assumed this would bring the conversation to an end.

"Oh," his father said brightly. "You should make one!"

Oliver stared at his plate. "Thanks. I'll think about it."

Now his father was musing aloud, tapping his pen on his paper. "You know who could help you make a kite?" he said.

"No," said Oliver, hoping desperately that his father wasn't about to offer.

"Your mother's uncle. Your great-uncle, I suppose. Name of Gilbert. I seem to recall he was a champion kite-smith, decades ago. Still lives in Windblowne somewhere, if I recall." His voice trailed off and he glanced back at his papers.

Oliver stared at his father, astonished. The fact that he had a relative who lived in Windblowne and was a former champion kitesmith, and that his parents had never bothered to mention it to him, was almost beyond belief. Almost. Only his parents, the biggest crackpots in Windblowne, could have failed to understand the importance of this fact.

His father, naturally, did not realize that he had just imparted to Oliver the most significant and startling information his son had ever received. His pen hovered over a page. Oliver knew he had to act quickly. "Dad?" he asked.

"Eh?" said his father, tapping the pen, lips pursed.

"Where does Great-uncle Gilbert live?"

"Windblowne, I believe."

Oliver stifled his frustration. "Yes, but where in Windblowne?"

"Not sure," his father said. The pen was scratching across paper again. "Never laid eyes on him. Hear he doesn't like people. Stormed off in a fury forty years ago over some kite business. Kicked up a giant fuss and got his name scrubbed from the records. Said he never wanted anything to do with anyone again. Hid himself away in a treehouse off in the forest and that was that. Quite the crackpot!"

His father bent over the page, and Oliver knew the conversation was over.

But he had learned everything he needed. Oliver knew exactly where Great-uncle Gilbert must have taken himself. The secret path! The mysterious person Oliver had tracked yesterday! There was a master kitesmith living near the path, and he was a relative, and Oliver had found him!

Cheered by his amazing powers of deduction, he attacked his breakfast. Surely his great-uncle could teach him how to make a champion kite. Oliver would convince him to help, appealing to family ties and so on. Oliver nearly choked, stuffing food in his mouth. He had to get up there and find his great-uncle.

He bolted out the front door and raced down the spiral stairs. There, to his horror, he saw his mother arguing with the mayor again. Oliver tried to slip by unnoticed.

"This is art! ART!" his mother was proclaiming to the

red-faced mayor. She had pushed all of her sculptures next to the Way. A few early Festival tourists had already gathered, their heads cocked quizzically.

"Your . . . art," fumed the mayor, his eyes darting toward the tourists, "will scare off all of our . . . *guests*! Move it!"

Oliver walked faster, but it was too late. His mother spotted him.

"Oliver!" said his mother with delight. "What do YOU think of my latest piece?" She pointed proudly to the last sculpture in line.

Oliver glanced at it dismally. Just like all the others, it was a meaningless jumble of metal and junk welded together. He wanted nothing to do with it. But his mother and the mayor were both watching him expectantly.

"It's, umm . . . tall," he offered. Now that he actually looked at it, he thought there might be something else about the sculpture, something interesting and familiar and a bit disturbing. Another brown leaf drifted by, and Oliver tracked it, his gaze flicking between leaf and sculpture.

His mother's face fell. "That's all?" she said.

Oliver groaned. Why was he standing here analyzing

statuary when there were kites to be crafted and a great-uncle to be found? "I don't know," he said in a rush. "I have to go." He raced away as the mayor beamed in triumph.

The Way was busier today than it had been all year. Windblowne was filling up for the Festival. Tourists were tramping up the mountain from the inns, looking curiously at everything.

Oliver found that without his flying clothes he blended in with the tourists. Normally his clothes would mark him as a Windblownian, and Festival tourists would look at him with respect (since they didn't know any better). But now they ignored him as they trudged, puffing with exertion. The only difference between them and Oliver was that he was not short of breath. A Windblownian could walk up and down the mountain all day without tiring.

Oliver passed one plodding, grumbling tourist after another. Some of the ones going up held kites; some of the ones coming down held pieces of kites. The handful whose kites were still intact were boasting to their friends. The others had forlorn faces with which Oliver could sympathize. Those with the broken kites would soon be buying new kites at one of Windblowne's kiteshops, which was exactly how the residents of Windblowne had planned things.

He was passing his favorite kiteshop now, the Volitant Dragon. Oliver thought that the Dragon had to be the greatest place on the mountain. It was built so high up in its oak you had to crane your neck to see it, and you might miss it were it not for the red wooden dragon that hung beside the Way, announcing boldly:

THE VOLITANT DRAGON
WINDBLOWNE'S TREASURE
— The World's Grandest Kites —

Vivid banners fluttered in the windows, advertising special Festival discounts. Oliver knew the discounts were a sham. All kiteshops doubled their prices during the Festival.

Just ahead stood the sentinel oaks, branches dipping. There came a break in the flow of tourists, and Oliver plunged into the brush.

He knew now the path must have been concealed intentionally. His great-uncle had done it to keep people away. Oliver was filled with admiration at the clever camouflage. How Oliver had ever noticed the path in the first place, he had no idea. For the first time in his life, he felt a rush of family pride. He supposed that if his great-uncle was a master kitesmith, then he must be good at a lot of other things, too. Oliver could not wait to meet him.

Halfway up the path, he began to search for the trail he had noticed yesterday, the one leading off into the forest's depths. It was not so easy to find. The mountain's little details changed from day to day as the wind did its work. Briefly, Oliver feared that he would not be able to locate it again. Then he noticed a flash of reflected light coming from beneath a few brown leaves, several feet off the path. He knelt, brushing the leaves aside, and gasped.

A golden kite charm lay half buried in leaves and dirt.

Ilia's charm! thought Oliver at first. Relief swept over him. *I've found it!* These small golden charms were common among the children of Windblowne. They were etched with the child's name and affixed to a kite before its first flight to bring good luck. Years ago, Oliver had bought one for himself, as his parents had not seen the point. He had promptly lost both his kite and the charm, as the wind tore the kite away and it flew—escaped, some said—over the oaks and away from Oliver forever.

He'd lost Ilia's charm too, or so he had thought. He lifted the charm gingerly and turned it over, looking for her name, but found instead:

Oliver

Oliver was stunned. He had found his own charm again, years after watching it disappear into the clouds. It seemed impossible—how could the charm be here, so many years later, lying right on the path? This could mean only one thing, Oliver decided. His luck had finally changed. He pocketed the charm with a grin. His great-uncle would help him and he would be a Festival hero after all. He swaggered down the side trail, grinning happily.

He soon found the chickens.

At first it was just one chicken, a large and startling one, fluffing out its wings and bawking at him. Oliver edged by rather fearfully, wondering what one did if a chicken attacked. He turned and saw another chicken, and another—a whole flock. Most of them, blessedly, were ignoring him, squabbling and pecking in a clear space in which vegetables were growing in a disorganized fashion. Here and there were rusting tools and scattered stacks of lumber. Oliver realized he must be close to his great-uncle's hidden treehouse. He scanned the oaks.

There it was, only two oaks away. The treehouse was built lower to the ground than most, and it blended in with its home oak in a way that made it difficult to spot if you weren't looking right at it. The whole thing was a madcap jumble, as though the builder had simply added rooms as he went along. A short staircase came straight down to the ground at a precarious angle.

Between the chickens and the rusting tools and the accidental garden, the scene reminded him uncomfortably of his own family's cluttered yard, except instead of being covered with abstract sculptures, it looked like the inside of a workshop that had been hit by a tornado.

He looked up through the branches of this healthy, giant oak, taking note of its subtle distinctions, adding it to a small gap in his map of which he had been unaware until now.

He could see that smoke was puffing from the chimney. Oliver jogged toward the staircase, a few chickens clucking angrily and scattering out of his way, then went up and rapped on the front door.

He heard what sounded like the scraping of a chair and fast-moving steps. Oliver waited for his knock to be answered.

And waited.

And waited some more. He knocked again.

No answer.

Oliver was beginning to get the distinct impression that there wouldn't be one. His great-uncle obviously didn't want to be bothered, but of course he did not realize that the person knocking was a member of his family. And not one of the weird ones, but one who had a normal and healthy interest in kites. Oliver knocked again, harder, and waited.

And waited.

Yes, his great-uncle's desire for privacy was understandable, but at the same time, the Festival would begin in three days, and Oliver had no time to waste. Pounding on the door any longer would simply be rude, however. Maybe he could wave at him through a window. Once Great-uncle Gilbert saw the family resemblance, he would surely welcome Oliver.

There was a balcony that ran around the first floor of the treehouse, with a number of windows in view. Oliver circled it, peering in. The first room was a kitchen. But the second . . .

Oliver sucked in his breath.

At least a dozen pristine kites were hanging from the ceiling; they looked as if they had never been flown. Any one of them could have taken the Festival prize for craftsmanship. Oliver had never seen such intricate designs and clever construction. The kites were not only beautiful, composed of delicate hand-painted silks, but they possessed advanced aeronautic features that showed they were intended to be operated only by the most skilled fliers. Scattered on several workbenches were another dozen kites in various stages of completion, and each looked as promising as the finished ones. Along the walls were sliding racks stuffed with more kites. Oliver longed to see them. They were all masterpieces, with one exception.

On the centermost workbench lay a flat, diamond-shaped kite, the type usually given as a first kite, to be flown only on nearly windless days. Oliver thought it wouldn't be a very nice kite to get, even as a first kite. Its silk was a lovely crimson, but otherwise the kite was art-less and unimaginative. The only interesting feature was its long tail, which had been haphazardly decorated with odd-shaped bits of cloth. The tail was coiled up next to the kite and was so long that it spilled down to the floor.

Suddenly one of the kite racks moved.

Startled, Oliver watched as it slid smoothly aside, re-vealing a dark, hidden room. Then, from another part of the workshop, an old man stepped into view.

Oliver ducked his head until his chin bumped the windowsill.

The old man, who had to be his great-uncle Gilbert, was squat and plump and dressed in a shabby purple robe. To Oliver's surprise, his great-uncle went imme-diately to the center workbench, snatched the crimson kite, and disappeared into the dark room that had just opened in the wall.

Oliver ducked lower as Great-uncle Gilbert emerged, no longer holding the kite. The old man hurried out of view. A few seconds later, the kite rack slid smoothly back into place.

Now Oliver was angry. He felt a bit guilty for spying on his great-uncle (he admitted that it had turned into spying), but then again, he would not have had to spy if Great-uncle Gilbert had simply answered the door like a normal person.

Oliver stalked back to the front door and gave it a resounding kick. The door shuddered in its frame. He waited a few seconds, then gave it another. And another. Determined not to tire, he reared back for an especially powerful kick.

Without warning, the door opened. Oliver, in mid-kick, fell backward. His great-uncle reached out and grabbed him just as he was about to tumble down the stairs.

"Hey!" Oliver yelled, swatting.

Great-uncle Gilbert released him, and Oliver looked the old man straight in the eye. He was only slightly taller than Oliver, and he was indeed very old, and very plump, and had a head full of wild gray hair.

He also had piercing brown eyes, and they were glaring right at Oliver. He reached out and gave Oliver a shove.

"So it's you again!" he growled. "I thought so. I told you never to come back. Go away!"

3

The front door slammed in Oliver's face, shaking the entire treehouse.

Oliver was too stunned to move. This was not exactly the joyous reunion of long-lost relations he had expected. For the first time in his life, his father might have been right about something. Great-uncle Gilbert was indeed a crackpot. The condition must run in the family.

Crackpot or not, the man knew a thing or two about kites. Oliver began to pound on the door to the beat of I-need-a-kite, I-need-a-kite.

After a minute the door flew open. In that minute, Great-uncle Gilbert had somehow managed to change into a pair of dirty blue overalls and a straw hat. He looked like someone who was trying to disguise himself as a farmer and doing a poor job of it. In one hand he clutched an elaborately carved walking stick and in the other an ornate clock. His face wore a regal scowl.

"I am going to feed the chickens," he announced royally. "Kindly remove yourself back to wherever it is you came from."

Great-uncle Gilbert strode forward, and Oliver, panting from all of the door kicking and pounding, dodged out of the way. His great-uncle sailed down the steps and Oliver followed, wondering if the chickens ate from a clock.

"What did you mean, 'It's you again'?" he demanded, catching his great-uncle at the bottom of the steps. "We've never met. I'm your grandnephew, Oliver!"

"So you are," replied Great-uncle Gilbert. "You can't fool me! Our visits are over. I trusted you with my secrets, and you betrayed me. Sorry you lost your kite charm—buy another!" They were halfway across the yard now. Chickens were scattering in all directions. Great-uncle Gilbert dropped the clock and took several sniffs, then turned in circles, cocking his head. "There's that smell again."

Oliver opened his mouth, intending to continue his argument. He had never been here before! And how did his great-uncle know about his kite charm? But then he smelled it, too. It was faint, at the very edge of his senses. Something that smelled wrong, or felt wrong, or both. Something full of decay.

The smell drew him toward an oak standing around one corner of the treehouse. Oliver had never seen this tree before, and into his map it went. The scent grew stronger. Behind him he could hear Great-uncle Gilbert sniffing and muttering.

"It's this oak," said Oliver.

He placed his hands on the trunk. The bark had an oddly soft feeling, as though the oak were somehow un-healthy. In the collective memory of Windblowne, the giant oaks were eternal. They were by far the largest, strongest trees anywhere in the world. None of them had ever shown the slightest sign of illness. Legend held that the oaks had been here, and would be here, as long as the mountain stood and the winds blew. So to look up the trunk of this oak and see its branches drooping, and its leaves showing a sick brown, left Oliver feeling a lit-tle sick as well. This oak must be the source of the dead leaves.

He heard crunching as Great-uncle Gilbert came

up behind him. Oliver turned to meet the man's nar-rowed eyes.

"You are not who I thought you were, are you?" whispered Great-uncle Gilbert.

"What?" said Oliver. "I—"

"You're *you,* not *him!*" said Great-uncle Gilbert, louder. "You look just alike! But of course, you would, wouldn't you?" He suddenly dropped his walking stick and shot forward, seizing Oliver's hands in his own. Oliver struggled to escape, but for such a plump old man, his great-uncle was shockingly strong.

Oliver's great-uncle's hands were not only strong, they were tremendously gnarled and callused, with scars from hundreds of tiny cuts. They were the hands of a master kitesmith after a lifetime of practicing his art.

Great-uncle Gilbert gripped Oliver's hands tightly, squeezing his knuckles, rubbing his fingers, examining his hands in every last detail.

At last his great-uncle released Oliver. He bent and picked up his walking stick. "So you're Oliver, from this mountain? I mean *this* one." He thumped the ground with the stick, his gaze focused on the far distance.

"Yes, that's right, Great-uncle Gilbert," said Oliver,

adopting the reassuring tones of a nurse. "I'm Oliver, your grandnephew, from Windblowne." *The man is mad through and through,* he thought.

"Well," said his great-uncle. "That is very interesting." He began to walk back to his treehouse, with Oliver following.

"I thought you needed to feed the chickens," said Oliver, looking at the abandoned clock.

"No, the chickens fend for themselves," Great-uncle Gilbert said grandly. "A clock is not a bucket of feed, my boy. I just wanted to get rid of you."

Great-uncle Gilbert mounted the stairs and proceeded through his front door. Oliver looked back at the sick oak worriedly. That would have to be another mystery to investigate, after the Festival. Oliver entered the treehouse, filled with determination.

"Great-uncle Gilbert," he began dramatically, "I have come to ask for your—"

The word *help* never escaped his lips as he stared stupidly at his great-uncle's living room.

The kite workshop, astonishing as it was, had nothing on this. His great-uncle appeared to be preparing for some sort of siege, or battle, or both. The right wall was bristling with fighting kites of all sizes, slick and fast and covered with razor hooks and edges. The back wall was stacked with water barrels and bundles of food. The left wall was covered with vast stretches of paper sketched all over with drawings of the treehouse and a lot of symbols and arrows that seemed to indicate elaborate plans for defense and counterattack against an aerial assault. And the room was rather dark, because the windows on the front wall were completely nailed over with heavy boards. Fortunately, a couple of oil lamps were burning. Oliver spotted barrels of surplus oil stacked in an open closet.

Great-uncle Gilbert was moving between windows, pounding in some more nails. "Ask for my what, my boy? Speak quickly, lad! I'm a touch busy at the moment." He gave one of the panels a resounding thump with his fist.

"Er . . . ," said Oliver feebly, trying to recover his impressive argument. "The Festival, and, uh . . . my kite . . ."

"Kites, is it?" said Great-uncle Gilbert thoughtfully. "Afraid I can't help you there. You must leave at once. It's far too dangerous for you here right now. Come back in, oh, a year or two. Or three. Yes, three would do nicely. Matters ought to be cleared up by then."

The blockade seemed complete. Great-uncle Gilbert nodded with satisfaction, then swept into the kitchen. Oliver followed.

They proceeded into the workshop, and Oliver's puzzlement increased. He could see that there was something completely out of place among the marvelous kites, something completely unexpected, not to mention completely boring. There was an entire shelf filled with his father's books.

Oliver could not have been more shocked if his great-uncle had suddenly sprouted wings and flown away. An entire shelf of those books! Just looking at it made Oliver feel tired. "Why do you have all of those?" Oliver asked suspiciously, pointing.

"Eh?" said Great-uncle Gilbert, sitting at a workbench. "Why wouldn't I? Fascinating stuff, those histories! Studying those old legends helped get me into this mess." He seemed rather gleeful about it.

Oliver shook his head. If he needed more evidence of his great-uncle's madness, here it was. "Those books are the most boring things in Windblowne," he explained.

"Yes, boring, so true," his great-uncle said. "In fact, they are so boring that you should rush off before it gets any more boring around here. Run home and hide under the bed is my advice, until everything blows over."

"Until what blows over?" demanded Oliver.

"I could tell you, my boy," replied Great-uncle Gilbert, "but you'd never believe me. None of 'em would! This town is full of people with limited imaginations."

Oliver shrugged. If Great-uncle Gilbert wanted to punish himself with tedious reading material, then Oliver couldn't stop him. He gazed around the workshop. Losing his own kiting gear last night had seemed like a setback, but Oliver could see that his great-uncle had the finest collection of kitesmithing supplies in Windblowne. There were barrels full of bamboo stalks cut to various sizes. Bolts of tightly woven silk were rolled up along the benches. And the spectacular kites that hung from the high ceiling would supply models of perfection that Oliver could follow as he built his new kite right here. Oliver was becoming positively giddy. Certainly Great-uncle Gilbert would come around once he understood how important Oliver's problems were.

"Great-uncle Gilbert," he said again, "I need a kite."

"No doubt!" Great-uncle Gilbert exclaimed. "You want to fly one of my kites in that farce of a Festival, don't you?" He shook his fist in the general direction of the crest. "Well, I know the rules! Most of them were written just to thwart me!"

"And the rules say you have to make your own kite," Oliver broke in. "I know."

Great-uncle Gilbert's snort expressed his contempt for anyone who would stoop to such a thing. "Well, the judges would know that any kites as amazing as mine could never have been made by you."

Whether this was true or not—and Oliver had to admit that it was—he was still more than a little hurt. "No," Oliver said desperately, his voice tight, "I have no intention of cheating. I only wanted you to teach me enough for me to make my own kite."

Great-uncle Gilbert seemed taken by surprise. "Er, sorry there, my boy," he said in gentle tones. "I didn't mean you'd cheat. It's just that I can tell a kitesmith. It's all in the hands. I've examined yours, and you don't have it in you." He scratched his chin thoughtfully. "Your talents," he said finally, "lie elsewhere."

"That's ridiculous," said Oliver. "You can't say that just from feeling someone's hands!" He felt tears coming and shook them away angrily.

Great-uncle Gilbert grimaced. "You think I'm a mad-man, don't you?" he growled. "Well, you're right. I am. My mind is filled with twists and turns and contradic-tions. But I do know one thing, and that's kites. Here, look at this one!" He snatched a kite from a nearby bench and thrust it at Oliver.

Oliver turned it around in his hands. The kite was made of slick black silk and a confusing tangle of oaken spars. Oaken spars! No one used oak for kite spars; it was far too heavy. Anyway, the thing hardly looked like a kite at all. Some of the spars came together in sharp points, and there were torn bits of colorful fabric cling-ing to them, and a few splinters.

"That," said Great-uncle Gilbert, "is one of my proud-est creations. It is a kite that eats other kites. Swoops right down on them and chomps them to bits. The fools banned it from competition! Be careful now," he said abruptly.

With a start, Oliver realized that he had somehow gotten his hand caught inside the kite. He pulled, but his hand was stuck fast.

"I can't get it out," said Oliver.

"You'd better," said Great-uncle Gilbert.

There was a sudden sharp pain in his hand, and Oliver yelped. He yanked hard, his hand burst free, and some of the spars snapped shut. He hurled the kite-eater away. It flew gracefully across the room, and Great-uncle Gilbert snatched it out of the air. "Good kite," he said approvingly, and placed it gently back on the workbench.

Oliver, stunned, said nothing, but rubbed his aching hand.

"You think that's something?" Great-uncle Gilbert snickered. "I don't even keep my best kite in here. I keep it hidden with my most valuable possessions, where *they* won't find it!"

Oliver wondered if he meant the plain crimson kite. If so, then it wasn't quite as amazing as his great-uncle claimed. He decided to humor the old man. "Where who can't find it, Great-uncle Gilbert?"

"*Them,*" said his great-uncle significantly. "Now shouldn't you be on your way?"

"I'm not leaving until you agree to help me with a Festival kite," said Oliver.

"Now, now, my boy," said Great-uncle Gilbert. He took another fighting kite from a rack and fiddled with its spars. "You need to forget about the Festival. I have!

Other matters of far greater importance, far greater danger, have presented themselves, and I will be very busy in days to come. You should occupy yourself with something else as well." He leaned toward Oliver, his voice falling to a whispered warning. "Something far, far away from the crest!"

This was too much for Oliver. First it was his parents, who were barely aware the Festival existed and certainly weren't going to do anything to help Oliver prepare for it. Now his great-uncle, who had once been a Festival champion and who owned the most splendid workshop and kites in all of Windblowne and thus in all the world, wasn't going to help him either. Oliver had opened his mouth to tell Great-uncle Gilbert exactly what he thought of his entire, useless family when he was interrupted by a thumping noise coming from behind the kite racks.

Great-uncle Gilbert spun about, ran to the racks, and threw his back against them. "Shhh!" he hissed over his shoulder. "Not now!"

Oliver gaped. "Who do you have in there?" he said accusingly.

"What are you talking about?" cried Great-uncle Gilbert. "I don't hear any thumping! Don't be preposterous!"

He turned his head to one side. "Stop that! Stop that right now!" he hissed again. "I'll let you out in a minute. I was just getting rid of him!" The steady *thump thump thump* continued without pause.

"No, you weren't!" snapped Oliver.

"Yes, I was!" shouted Great-uncle Gilbert, and Oliver found himself propelled out of the workshop, his great-uncle's hands gripping his shoulders. He was pushed through the living room and out the front door. Oliver staggered as his great-uncle released him at the top of the steps. He turned. Great-uncle Gilbert was blocking the doorway, breathing heavily. The steady thumping could still be heard behind him.

"Well," his great-uncle said quickly, "that was a lovely visit, thank you. We shouldn't do it again anytime soon. And you must avoid the crest at all costs. That's how *he* came through, and it would be a dangerous thing indeed for *you* to run into *him*. Regards to your parents." And with that, he slammed the door. Oliver heard running footsteps fading away.

Oliver sagged against the door. His final hopes had rested in someone who turned out to be a complete lunatic. Lunacy must run in the family. His mother was headed that way too, and Oliver supposed he would be next.

He turned wearily and plodded down the steps. Now what? Oliver looked at the abandoned clock, ticking remorselessly away in the cluttered yard.

The day had become cold and gray while he was indoors, and chill winds blew over him as he trudged off. He pulled his jacket closer. The winds made eerie sounds as they threaded through the oaks, bringing with them that scent of decay from the strange, sick oak, as well as the rattling patter of its dead leaves. Oliver was filled with foreboding. The giant oaks were waving their branches as the winds came through, and it looked to Oliver as though they were waving helplessly.

Oliver shook it off. He didn't intend to go crazy like the rest of his family. Not yet anyway. He was determined to enter the Festival somehow and show them all.

He turned down the hidden path toward Windswept Way, toward home. He walked quickly. He did not like the sound of the winds in the oaks, wailing and mournful. Oliver's walk turned into a jog, and then he found himself running for the shelter and warmth of home, chased by the cry of the winds.

4

That night, Oliver quivered in bed, wide-eyed and sleep-less. Outside, the winds howled. The treehouse creaked and groaned. Oliver thought the winds sounded angry enough to rip the treehouse from the tree's embrace and send it spinning away. Oliver longed to run across the hall and place his hands on the trunk to reassure himself of its solidity and strength, but he didn't dare leave his bed.

He could not fathom how his parents slept through this unusually powerful windstorm, but they seemed completely undisturbed. Oliver's heart pounded and his mind raced. He was covered in sweat, his sheets twisted into knots.

I'm going to light a candle, he thought. He threw the covers aside. *I'm going to light every candle I can find.*

But then

BAM

something crashed against the treehouse so close to him that the wall shook and Oliver nearly screamed. He pulled the covers back over his head. And then a sound came again,

tap tap tap

like a person rapping on the shutter. He lifted his head cautiously from beneath the blankets. That had really sounded like

tap tap tap

someone knocking to get in. But no one could possibly be out at night, sitting on an oak branch, rapping on the window next to Oliver's bed. He waited for several seconds.

TAP TAP TAP

Oliver rolled over and yanked the curtains aside. Moonslight flashed on something flickering among the lashing branches. *No,* he thought, *it can't be....*

He pulled up the window.

The winds invaded with a roar and nearly threw him from his bed. He clung to the windowsill as Great-uncle Gilbert's kite, the simple long-tailed crimson kite, came crashing in, slamming into walls and bouncing off the floor and ceiling. It thrashed uncontrollably as Oliver struggled to close the window. Then the winds slackened briefly, the kite flew over Oliver's head and out into the night, and the window slammed home.

Oliver fell back on his bed in astonishment. Somehow, improbably, the winds had gotten hold of the hidden kite. It was a colossal piece of luck. Now he possessed something his great-uncle wanted. Or he would possess it, anyway, as soon as he chased down the wayward kite.

This is a really stupid idea, said a little voice in the back of Oliver's head. But Oliver had ignored that voice before, and he was going to ignore it now. He fished his rugged flier's outfit from under the bed, dressed quickly, and raced from the room.

Using the front door was out of the question. With the winds hammering at the walls, opening the door would invite disaster. Oliver went straight to the emergency wind hatch in the tiny room off the kitchen. He lifted the trapdoor and put one foot on the first rung of the ladder.

Below him the ladder descended through the protected wind shaft and then along the trunk into battering darkness. He wavered. The odds of catching the kite were terribly low, and the odds of breaking a leg were terribly high. Should he really do this? The plan was sheer madness. *Runs in the family,* thought Oliver. Flattening himself against the trunk, he descended swiftly and dropped into the open winds.

He braced himself against the turbulence, his back to his solid home oak. The world was wild around him. Everything not rooted firmly in the ground had been lifted and thrown. The scream of the winds as they tore through the oaks was deafening, as though the night had life and was warning him back. Trembling, Oliver recalled childhood tales of wicked boys and girls who had been carried off by the winds, never to be seen again.

But I must have the kite, thought Oliver. *I'll catch it and come straight home. And I'm not going anywhere near the crest.*

He staggered away from the oak. The moment he abandoned the oak's solidity he became disoriented, all sense of direction lost in the churning night. The winds came up from behind and pushed him forward, and he fought back, peering about for the kite. At first he feared that it might have been blown too far away to catch, but then he spied a crimson blur.

The kite was flitting among a line of oaks. None of them were oaks that Oliver recognized. For a confused instant, he felt as though he had stepped into another world. Seven trees stood before him, looming in the dark; seven anguished silhouettes, broken and tortured. Then the winds shifted, the shadows changed, and Oliver realized he was not looking at seven oaks racked in pain but seven sculptures lining Windswept Way—his mother's art.

His map restored, he ran, stumbling as the winds lashed him. His exposed face stung as twigs and leaves became missiles in the driving winds. He could barely keep the kite in sight, with all of the weird and distracting shadows changing each moment. He saw that it had moved upward on the Way. He gave chase, but the kite bobbed just out of reach, flying tantalizingly close and then darting away just as Oliver closed his fingers.

Suddenly the kite ducked sideways, into the forest. They had come to the secret path, and the kite had flown between the sentinels as though it knew the way. In fact, the kite had been flying in an oddly deliberate fashion all along.

With a crash, Oliver went headlong into the brush.

The kite reached the turn to Great-uncle Gilbert's treehouse and slipped off the path. Oliver slipped after it.

Then light exploded through the oaks, a brilliant split-second flash that lit the forest in stark relief.

Oliver was momentarily blinded. When he opened his eyes again, the kite had disappeared.

He ran through the trees, moonslight spilling across his path, until he reached the clearing.

He arrived in the midst of a battle.

The seconds that followed were entirely confusing. Oliver saw Great-uncle Gilbert flying two of the bladed fighting kites, one in each hand, with astonishing skill. The kites were cutting tight circles on their short tow-lines. The old man was fending off three other kites, dark, speed-blurred shapes. But who was flying those kites? Oliver couldn't see anyone else in the clearing.

"Great-uncle Gilbert!" Oliver shouted.

Great-uncle Gilbert glanced over. "Oliver!" he cried. "No!"

The distraction was all the dark kites needed. Two of them dove in, and Great-uncle Gilbert's fighting kites disappeared in snapping spars and shreds of silk. The third attacked Great-uncle Gilbert directly, hooking onto his robe. Oliver whirled around. Where were the fliers?

A shout of pain came from the treehouse. Then someone, a boy, burst through the front door and pounded down the wooden steps.

The other boy was dressed in a flier's outfit, exactly like Oliver's. His arms were full of folded kites.

"Go!" cried the boy.

There was another dazzling flash.

Oliver's vision spun and wavered, and it seemed as though he were seeing double. Two treehouses, two of every oak. He looked at the other boy. He was seeing double there, too. When he looked the boy in the face, he could have sworn that the face he saw was his own.

Two dark kites flew to the boy, hooking onto his gloves.

There was another blinding flash, and for a minute Oliver staggered about the clearing, groping, completely blind.

When his vision recovered, the clearing was empty. He saw no sign of Great-uncle Gilbert or any of the kites, or the other boy.

He looked toward the treehouse.

The front door was wide open, dim light spilling from within. Every few seconds something blew from inside— candlesticks, papers, odd bits of furniture—filling the air with swirling debris.

From within the treehouse there came a tremendous crash.

5

Oliver raced up the steps.

Inside, the treehouse was in shambles. The winds had reduced everything to pure chaos. Oliver pushed against the door and shoved it closed. He looked around the living room. His great-uncle's supplies had been knocked over, bits of the fighting kites had been smashed around, and the wall once covered with battle plans now had only a few scraps remaining. One of the barricaded windows had been bashed open. There were several long, deep slashes in the fallen board, as though a powerful animal had raked its claws across it. Somehow, an oil lamp tucked in one corner had survived, its weak flame casting a weirdly flickering glow. Oliver hurriedly retrieved it.

"Great-uncle Gilbert!" Oliver cried. "Hullo!"

A terrific ruckus came from the workshop. Oliver ran toward the sound, nearly tripping on an overturned stool, and burst into the room.

"Great-uncle . . . ," Oliver began, but the words died away. He set the lamp aside. His great-uncle was not here, and neither were most of his kites. The shelves were empty, the workbenches cleared—even the kite racks stood open and bare. Only two kites remained— the crimson kite, which was being madly chased around the workshop, and the ravenous black kite-eater, which was doing the chasing.

Oliver leapt. He fell upon the kite-eater and pinned it to the floor. Pain shot through his hand as the kite-eater caught him in its jaws. Oliver cried out and pulled; the kite-eater heaved and struggled. He looked desperately for a weapon. Nearby, on the floor, he spotted a book. Not just any book but a heavy, familiar, boring book. Just the book, in fact, to trap a kite-eater. Oliver grabbed for it with one hand, hauled it over with a tremendous grunt, and rolled aside, pulling it onto the kite-eater as he went.

He had finally found a use for one of his father's massive tomes. It made the perfect restraint for an aggressive kite. Oliver crawled backward, panting from the unexpected wrestling match. At first he feared that even this book would not be enough to hold down the kite-eater, but no matter how much it twisted and fought and snapped its jaws, it could not escape the sheer weight of *The Social and Cultural History of the Lower Warfeld Valley in Late Mid-Age Macherino.* Oliver knew the feeling well.

The crimson kite collapsed onto a workbench, seemingly exhausted, its sails heaving.

"Great-uncle Gilbert!" shouted Oliver.

He quickly searched the rest of the treehouse. There was no sign of his great-uncle.

He stopped in the living room, looking at what was left of the strange maps and overturned barrels. The crimson kite had recovered and was swooping in agitated circles around and around the room. Oliver looked out the bashed-in window into the windblown night. Feeling useless, he picked up the fallen board and shoved it back into place.

grrrrrr

He heard a noise, like a faint grinding, almost as though something were . . . chewing.

Oliver ran back into the workshop.

The kite-eater was still pinned under the enormous

book, or rather, part of the book. It had already managed to chew through some of it. Bits of torn paper surrounded the abused book and the kite-eater, which snapped its jaws savagely when Oliver entered.

"Oh no you don't!" said Oliver sharply. Setting down the lamp, he ran to the shelf of his father's books and reached up for the next one. As he hauled it down, he noticed the title—*The Mountain Before Windblowne*—just before the book slipped from his grasp and crashed to the floor, narrowly missing his foot.

Gasping with the effort, Oliver lugged the book over to the kite-eater and threw it on top of the pile. Then another book. Then another. The kite-eater gnashed its jaws. "Sorry," Oliver panted, "but you're not eating that kite."

The crimson kite was peeking into the workshop. "You can come in," Oliver said. "I've got the kite-eater trapped."

Oliver had always talked to his kites, but he'd never had the impression that one of them might be listening. Or if they were, it was only so they could do the exact opposite of whatever he asked. For example, "No, please, not in the tree" was interpreted to mean "Please dive directly into that tree," or "Watch out for the crowd of people" meant

"Smash into the crowd of people in order to humiliate me as much as possible."

And that record remained unchallenged, as the crimson kite shook dubiously and refused to enter.

Oliver looked around. Most of his great-uncle's beautiful kites had been stolen. They'd apparently been stolen by that other boy, who in the confusion and blinding flashes had looked just like him. Somehow the boy had been able to make his escape under the cover of those flashes, and he'd managed to kidnap Great-uncle Gilbert and thoroughly ransack his workshop in the process. Everything of value was gone.

Almost everything, Oliver realized. The kite rack that concealed Great-uncle Gilbert's secret room, where he kept his most valuable possessions, was still in place.

Oliver pushed and pulled in every direction, but the rack refused to yield. He took a hammer that had fallen to the floor and tried to pry the rack from the wall. He even gave it a few kicks, which resulted in nothing but a minute or two of hopping around in pain. The kite-eater seemed to be enjoying the spectacle—it had stopped chewing on the book and was watching Oliver avidly. Oliver had a sense that it was grinning at him. "Stop that," he ordered, "unless you want another one of those books on you." The kite-eater quickly resumed chewing.

Oliver inspected the kite rack. From all appearances, it was part of a solid wall. He thought back to what he had seen through the window. His great-uncle had not actually been anywhere near the rack when it slid aside. He had been somewhere else in the room, somewhere Oliver couldn't see from where he had been crouched. Turning the oil lamp up to its brightest level, Oliver surveyed the workshop.

Across the room, just above the shelf from which Oliver had pulled all the books, he spotted the tiniest depression in the wall. A hidden button, nearly invisible.

Oliver gave a whoop of triumph. "I'm brilliant," he said to the kite-eater. The kite-eater replied by snapping at his ankle as he passed by. Oliver pushed the button. There was a click, and behind him the kite rack slid smoothly aside.

Oliver was disappointed to discover that the secret room was more of a secret closet. It was small and terribly dusty. On the back wall was a peg on which a single kite could be hung. Below that were a few dust-coated items sitting on shelves.

One of these items was a small chest, ornately carved. Oliver ran his finger over the intricate designs, leaving a trail in the thick dust. He tried to open the chest, but it was locked.

The next shelf held a soft velvet pillow, upon which lay a handvane. Though the pillow was covered in dust, the handvane was not. Oliver could tell right away that this was one of his great-uncle's personal creations. It was carved from oak, and though it looked delicate and fine, Oliver suspected that it could stand up under the fiercest windstorm. He lifted it reverently and fastened it onto his wrist.

As it snapped into place, he felt a moment's hesitation. Was this stealing? No, he decided—this was preserving. After all, Great-uncle Gilbert's abductor might return for further pillaging. Oliver ought to protect one of the old man's most valuable possessions. The fact that Oliver needed a new handvane was just a coincidence.

The only other thing in the closet was a book, which lay on the lowest shelf. It was not one of his father's books, though it was equally enormous. The cover was rough and leathery. There had once been a title, but it was now too faded to read. The book had a musty odor, and dull jewels were set into the cover. Oliver reached out gingerly and lifted the cover, the spine creaking quietly. He held the oil lamp close.

On the yellowed first page were words written in a style so elegant and ancient that Oliver could scarcely read them:

❧ MYTHS & FOLK–LORE OF WINDBLOWNE ☙

Fascinated, Oliver turned the delicate pages. The book was filled with lavish illustrations and dense type, most of which made no sense to him.

He lifted the heavy book to look closer, and it fell open to a page that Oliver could see had been consulted often. The margins of this and the following pages were filled with tiny notes and sketches drawn in a loose and rambling hand that Oliver suspected was Great-uncle Gilbert's. At the top of the first page in this section it said:

The Whispering Oaks

Oliver leafed through it in wonder. Here were pictures of things he recognized. There were many drawings of tall oak trees, including his home oak and the oak that held the Volitant Dragon, though they all looked odd without treehouses in them. Next to one of these drawings was a passage that seemed to have particularly interested Great-uncle Gilbert. It was underlined, and the notes beneath it were more legible than the others. Oliver read:

> . . . but legends concerning the giant oaks of Windblowne remain pleasant stories for children, and for fools and madmen as well, who claim that in the whisper of winds passing through the oaks, a great mystery is revealed.

Underneath this, in his great-uncle's scrawled hand, Oliver read:

> "the winds do not whisper . . .
> but if you do whisper, O winds, then
> whisper to me,
> of oaks which dwell across the worlds."

Oliver shuddered, remembering the despairing cries he had imagined on the winds. *A language for fools and madmen.*

He felt something nudge his arm, and looked down. It was the crimson kite, gently brushing him, its tail swirling clear of the kite-eater's jaws.

He slammed the book shut. The kite fled from the workshop.

Oliver followed, pressing the button once more as he went. He heard the kite rack slide closed behind him.

When he reached the living room, he found the crimson kite smacking itself against the front door.

"You're going to hurt yourself," said Oliver. "Here."

He opened the door, and the kite flew outside into the night, then paused, hovering, its long tail beckoning.

"Forget it!" shouted Oliver into the winds, thinking of the long slashes on the barricade, and the dark fighting kites. "I'm not following you anywhere else tonight. It's too dangerous!"

The kite rose higher, shaking frantically.

"Come home with me," pleaded Oliver, feeling guilty despite himself. "We'll alert the Watch at dawn."

But the kite shuddered in the turbulent winds and flew no closer.

"Fine!" he shouted. "I'm going home. Great-uncle

Gilbert told me to stay away anyway. He doesn't want my help!"

Oliver came down the steps, leaning into the winds, as the kite danced backward, lashing its tail.

"I'm not scared or anything! It's just that I've got the Festival to think about!"

He tried to march onward impressively, but before he could take his first impressive step, he heard a *whoosh,* and then the kite was in his face, beating its sails against him. He tried to grab the kite, but it slipped around him, striking at him. Oliver ran down the path, arms over his head, the kite in close pursuit.

He stopped. The kite drifted menacingly before him, blocking the path. Oliver thought longingly of his safe, warm bed. He had to come up with a way out of this. The last thing he wanted to do, given his reputation, was run through Windblowne being chased by a kite.

"Look," he said to the kite, "be reasonable."

The kite hovered warily.

"There's nothing I can do to help Great-uncle Gilbert, whatever's happened to him, even if I wanted to. Even if he had trusted me. Even if he hadn't almost shoved me down the stairs and set his kite-eater on me and"—

Oliver realized he was getting carried away—"and everything else."

The kite buzzed, tail lashing like a whip.

"You heard Great-uncle Gilbert," Oliver said. "I don't have any talents. I'll never be a kitesmith. My great-uncle wants nothing to do with me, and neither does anyone else!"

The kite's sails sagged mournfully.

"So that's it," Oliver continued uncertainly. This had been easier when the kite fought back. "If you don't want to come with me, then fine. I promise to tell the Watch all about this."

The kite drooped away. It drooped past Oliver and back up the path. Oliver watched it go. It appeared determined to fly on, whether Oliver was coming or not.

"Fine!" declared Oliver, without conviction. He turned toward home. The path ahead swirled with fallen leaves. A few low, bare oak branches draped the path, their shadows tracing the ground.

A distant sound came to his ears—an immense wave of wind, far off but rolling closer. The world seemed to gather itself. The treetops stilled, oak leaves settled to earth, and Oliver held his breath. He knew this sound. A windburst was coming, and a big one.

Before he felt it, he could see it, as oaks in the distance began to thrash wildly, sending up clouds of leaves to join the wave.

Oliver braced for impact as the wave hit. He threw up his hands to protect his face when the leaf-cloud enveloped him, rushing past.

The winds pummeled and fought, and he fought back, pushing with all of his strength. Step by step, he battled forward.

He risked a glance back.

The crimson kite, buffeted by the winds, was drifting heavily up the path. In moments, it was lost to Oliver's view.

Oliver dropped his hands. The winds rose again, and thousands of oak branches shook together. Then the wind-wave passed, and Oliver listened as it rolled away across the mountain.

He fell to his knees, exhausted from his struggle with the winds.

I win, he thought. *I can go home.*

But he didn't go. He crouched there, hearing the weird and distant dying voices of the windburst.

He plucked a few dead leaves from his sweater. Looking at them, he could see that they were not all from the sick oak. One of them came from a sentinel, and another from the oak across the Way from his own home oak.

He looked at these leaves, and he remembered the soft feel of the sick oak's bark, and he remembered the way Great-uncle Gilbert had shouted "No!" and looked at him, and how that distraction had resulted in his great-uncle's defeat and disappearance. Something was very wrong with the oaks, and he had a feeling that Great-uncle Gilbert had been trying to do something about it.

And all this with the Festival only two days away.

Oliver groaned, then ran after the kite. When he caught up, it whirled about in surprise, then spun happily in the air.

This is madness, thought Oliver, and in a way that sealed it for him. He was mad like his great-uncle and his parents.

"All right," he said with resignation. "If you know where Great-uncle Gilbert is, then take me there."

The kite shot back up the path, and Oliver followed, buffeted by the winds. He ran all the way back up the path, following the lashing tail, past the turn to his great-uncle's house—and then, in horror, he realized where the kite was leading him. The crest.

In moments they reached the oakline, where the path emerged onto the crest. The kite stopped, hovering, and Oliver stopped too, just a few feet away. He clutched at a nearby branch and squinted as dust and debris from the raging winds swarmed over him.

On the crest, the grass was bent flat as a sheet, and the moonslight stabbed down through a chaotic cloud of unbridled power, a screaming maelstrom where the protection of the oaks ended and the night winds leveled everything. Oliver felt as though he were staring into the maw of an invincible creature bent on total destruction.

The crimson kite dipped down like a flier preparing to leap.

"Please," Oliver begged, screaming. "Don't! You'll be destroyed!" He held out one hand in supplication. "Please."

The kite shook proudly, sails snapping, and flew into the storm.

Oliver screamed and lunged for the tail, but too late. It flickered just ahead of his hand, and was gone.

As he stumbled across the oakline, the night winds knocked him flat, driving the breath from his body. Ahead he could see the kite, somehow resisting utter destruction, flying defiantly toward the peak.

Then the winds picked him up and threw him as though he were a scrap of silk. They slammed him into a nearby oak, knocking the breath from him and causing him to see a dazzling array of stars. He managed to crawl around to the lee side of the trunk, away from the full force of the winds. The crimson kite, illuminated by moonslight at the peak, turned in circles as though searching for something. It spied Oliver and flew at him.

The kite came to an abrupt halt only a few feet away. Oliver did not understand how the kite could fly in the night winds, but he didn't care, for the kite's tail was now dangling in front of him tantalizingly. He leapt and found a fistful of silk. He whooped in triumph as the tail lashed itself around his forearm like a striking whip.

The whoop died as the kite began to drag him, powered by the irresistible force of the night winds, onto the crest.

"I can't!" screamed Oliver over the roar of the winds. Bits of leaf and twig blistered his cheeks. He dug in his heels and fought back, knocked from one side to another as the winds beat at him. He pulled as hard as he could. But with the night winds powering the kite, Oliver couldn't win.

The savage winds tearing at him, he struggled up the crest, expecting at any moment to be hurled away. But no matter how ferociously the winds blew, the kite held firm, pulling him higher. He passed the jumping marker, hardly noticing it. His mind was filled with cautionary tales told to Windblowne's children, stories of how the night winds could take a piece of straw and drive it into the trunk of an oak like an arrow—or into the body of a foolish child who defied the night winds.

The kite had nearly reached the peak, dragging Oliver just behind. He felt nearly at the end of his strength. The kite loomed over him. The two moons gleamed beyond.

For one instant, the night winds slackened, just enough for Oliver to gather himself for one last pull.

Then the winds blasted back in all of their fury. The tail snapped taut and pain tore through Oliver's shoulder. The kite shot into the sky, and Oliver went with it.

Terror flooded him. He had never learned to kite jump, and yet here he was, leaping out from the crest, legs kicking. Already he was too high to let go of the kite, even if he could. His only chance was to hang on and attempt a safe landing.

The kite and Oliver rose rapidly, the barren ground racing below. Oliver saw moonslight glinting off the granite marker.

A new thought replaced the terror: *I'm going to come close to the record.*

Now he was flying faster, still rising.

I'm going to BREAK the record!

The granite marker sped by in a blur. Oliver would have yelled in triumph if certain death had not been seconds away. He was hurtling straight toward the oaks, a hundred feet off the ground. The kite continued to rise. The oaks came near, then passed beneath them, the tips of their highest branches brushing Oliver's legs.

Looking down, he saw the treehouses of Windblowne, now far below, and a light escaping through the trees where someone, woken by the winds, moved restlessly, unable to sleep.

Then they passed upward into a chilling mist, and Oliver could see no more.

6

Oliver had always admired carrier kites, immense kites large enough for a person to sit in and be flown high above the mountain. He had admired their daring passengers even more. Though carrier kites were controlled from the ground by teams of fliers, it nevertheless took nerves of oak to soar at such altitude, held aloft only by silk and bamboo and the work of your own hands. But Oliver had now achieved an entirely new understanding of altitude. From where he soared, he would be looking down at any carrier kite that had ever flown. And from the ground, Oliver and the kite would be no more than a speck in the sky.

Oliver thought he ought to feel terrified. Here he was, clinging to the tail of a small kite, miles above the ground in the midst of the most ferocious windstorm he had witnessed in a short life filled with ferocious windstorms. Not only was he in ridiculous danger, but he was also not the boy best equipped to bring this flight to a successful conclusion, one that did not involve breaking every bone in his body and becoming the posthumous laughingstock of all Windblowne.

And yet, he wasn't frightened. Instead, an unfamiliar feeling surged through him: happiness. He tried a few experimental screams of joy, which were snatched away on the winds.

Perhaps it was that the night winds carried him so smoothly, as though wrapped in a blanket of air, although they must have been hurtling at unheard-of speeds. The crimson kite had lashed its tail firmly around his forearm.

They seemed to be flying through a cloud. Oliver wished he could see the stars, or the lights of passing towns racing by below, or anything at all besides the faint glow of enveloping mist illuminated by the moons.

Still, he was flying higher and farther than anyone had ever flown, he was sure, and he began formulating big plans for his triumphant return to Windblowne. He had broken about seven different records that he could think of, and had set about five others that he had invented along the way. Twelve new records! His homecoming would be grand, even if it took him a few weeks to get back from wherever he landed. He wondered where they would put the granite marker, which would now be emblazoned with his name. The new placement would be many leagues from Windblowne, which was a shame, but at least this record was sure to be unbreakable. In the absence of the marker, Oliver would just have to remind everyone of the accomplishment himself. And in a distant town somewhere, people would gather around the granite marker and ask themselves, "Who was this Oliver, this bold adventurer who descended from the skies? What sort of brilliant flying was required to—"

Abruptly, Oliver noticed that he was no longer being pulled directly behind the kite. He was not flying but dangling, a tiny figure lost in the vast sky. The winds were slowing. Dawn was arriving with surprising swiftness. He became conscious of the miles of empty space below him. Without the strength of the night winds, the kite would not be able to keep both of them aloft.

"Shouldn't we begin preparations for landing?" Oliver

shouted. He attempted a few experimental tugs on the tail, but the kite took no notice.

A brighter glow spread through the mist. "Kite," said Oliver firmly, hoping that for once a kite would listen to him. "Landing time. Let's go." He gave another tug. No response.

Then the kite began to sink, slowly at first, then faster. Oliver was sweating now and kicking his legs. The winds that had carried him along gently for hours were now rushing straight up past him, and not gently. He thought of a thirteenth record he was about to set—first flier to be squashed while flying a kite. No one in Windblowne would be surprised that Oliver had set that record. They could plant the granite marker on the spot where he met his violent end.

Then, in a smooth, silent rush, the mist cleared.

Oliver could see the ground approaching with alarming speed.

They were falling through the last wisps of the dying night winds, straight toward the crest of another mountain.

Since there were no other mountains anywhere near Windblowne, Oliver knew they must have flown very far indeed. He was going to die, alone, on a strange and faraway mountain, a mere splotch on the landscape, with no one to document the twelve records he had just set. At least he would avoid the public embarrassment of record number thirteen.

Oliver shut his eyes and waited for impact.

There was a loud snap, and pain shot through him—but the snap was only the kite's sails going taut once more, and the pain was only from his beleaguered shoulder. Oliver opened his eyes and saw the ground rushing up below his feet. He tucked his legs, hit the ground hard, and rolled forward onto his back. He looked up at the kite, which hovered over him, dancing back and forth as the final night winds curled away.

"Very funny," Oliver said.

The kite fluttered proudly.

Oliver lay there for a minute, glorying in the feel of being alive and on solid ground and in possession of an intact skeleton. He had braved the greatest heights ever achieved by a flier. No one needed to know how terrified he had been at the end.

In the thrill of the flight, he had almost forgotten why he had followed the kite in the first place.

"So where's Great-uncle Gilbert?" he said to the kite. "Where are we, anyway?"

But the kite was simply flying around him in anxious circles.

He rolled onto his stomach and climbed achingly to his feet, rubbing his arm, which burned where the kite had unlashed its tail just before landing. He wondered how many leagues he'd flown—ten? a hundred? Was he in a new land? Would the people here speak a strange language? Would they grasp the epic scope of his accomplishments? Would they object to the new placement of the granite marker?

Oliver looked around, the light of dawn revealing everything—and cried out in dismay.

He'd thought he had shattered half the records in the book. But now he could see he was standing right on the Windblowne crest, exactly at the point from which he'd taken off. There was the granite marker, far off, glinting in the morning sun. He hadn't set the record after all—unless it was the record for the shortest jump of all time. He wondered if there was a record for the longest jump for the least distance, for surely he'd broken that record many times over. They must have been going in circles the entire time.

Oliver shot the kite a disgusted look. "Couldn't you have at least set me down a little past the marker?"

The kite's sails drooped sadly.

"No, it was a great flight, really," said Oliver hastily. "I just wish we could do it during the day." He imagined turning circles around the crest, waving at admiring crowds of tourists arriving for the Festival. . . .

Speaking of which . . . the crest ought to be busy with preparations. Though dawn had only just broken, he ought to have seen the first trickle of fliers arriving for a few precious hours of practice. He ought to have seen workers arriving to set up reviewing stands for tourists who couldn't bear to sit on the grass. He ought to have seen Festival officials arriving to put up banners that snapped in the wind, announcing the schedule of events, and carts arriving full of food to sell.

But Oliver could see none of those things, and the only sound he could hear was the light whistle of the cool winds of dawn, sounding strange to him even though he had heard them so many times. This morning they seemed louder, more piercing, and somehow he felt they were even giving him a slight headache.

"Let's go," he said to the kite, which was still flying

those anxious circles. He held out his hand. "Come on! We've got to go find help."

Shockingly, it obeyed instantly, flying directly to him. He tucked the kite under his arm. The kite's long tail whipped out and wrapped around his waist, and the kite huddled next to his body, pressing against him. It seemed to be shivering, too.

As he walked toward the secret path, his unease increased. He realized that he had not heard a single bird-call. Normally, when dawn broke, birds would fill the air with chirping and song. But Oliver heard nothing but the unsettling whistle of the winds, which pierced right through him and left behind a growing headache. And under his arm, the kite was now noticeably trembling.

"What's wrong?" Oliver asked irritably.

He stopped. He'd reached the entrance to the secret path.

But the secret path was secret no longer.

Someone had cleared away all of the brush that had disguised the entrance. And the rest of the path had been cleared too, as though it were now a common thorough-fare. Oliver, feeling possessive, considered covering it up again, but he couldn't see any of the cleared brush nearby.

Oliver felt the kite vibrating under his arm. "Would you relax?" he said anxiously, tightening his grip.

Then he noticed the strings.

They were up high in the oaks—you had to look up to see them—and they weren't really strings exactly, but Oliver did not know what else to call them. They were long strands of something thin and black, and they were strung from oak to oak, fastened to the trunks somehow, winding off in all directions.

Oliver stood thinking for several minutes. The kite huddled next to him, shaking all the while.

No fliers on the crest. No Festival preparations. No birds. The secret path revealed. The black strings in the trees.

A couple of dead leaves drifted by. Oliver snatched them from the air. He knew them immediately. One came from the sick oak next to Great-uncle Gilbert's treehouse. The other, from the Volitant Dragon's oak.

The leaves looked exactly as Oliver expected them to, besides being prematurely dead. The rest of the world, though, seemed subtly different. The grass was heavy and green, more so than usual. The blue sky was empty, not only of birds and kites, but there was also no sign of the cloud from which Oliver had flown. The world had changed in a hundred different ways—its scent, its light, and many other things Oliver could sense but not identify. Nothing looked, felt, or smelled quite as it should.

Especially the winds, with their shrill, keening, painful cry.

The quivering kite pressed itself ever more closely to Oliver.

"Where are we?" whispered Oliver.

In the sky, something moved.

On the other side of the crest, a distant kite had risen. With the peak between them, Oliver could not see who had launched it. But the graceful movements indicated an expert flier.

And then that kite, circling high and smoothly, flapped its wings.

Oliver blinked and peered harder. Flapping wings? It couldn't be a kite. Now that it had flown closer, it looked more like a hawk, hunting its prey.

The crimson kite pulled violently, yanking Oliver aside.

"Ouch! What?" he said, struggling to hold his ground.

A second hawk had risen to join the first. While Oliver watched, a third rose from the oaks to join the others.

Suddenly the crimson kite stopped pulling and crept under Oliver's arm. It huddled there, eerily still.

The hawks circled, circled, in the bright blue sky. The circles brought them closer to Oliver, until they were nearly over his head. He developed a distinctly hypnotized, mouselike feeling as he realized that he was utterly still too, just like the crimson kite.

And as they drew near, he realized they were not hawks.

They were kites after all, and he'd seen their dark shapes before. They were the fighting kites that had attacked Great-uncle Gilbert. Silhouetted against the sky, they looked exactly like hawks.

The fighters dove.

Oliver threw himself to the ground as the crimson kite shot away. The three fighters rocketed after it. In the morning sunlight, something within their sails flashed and gleamed in a very unkitelike way. The crimson kite streaked into the forest, the fighters close behind.

Oliver scrambled to his feet, blood pounding. He raced toward the peak for a better view, and heard voices.

He slid to a halt a few yards short of the peak. Voices rose from the other side, coming closer:

"It's back! The hunters spotted it; they—"

A second voice interrupted. Oliver could not make out the words. The voice was crackled and muffled as though the owner's head were wrapped in silk and he had a terrible cold.

The first voice spoke again, sounding out of breath. "Yes, sir, I'll find it right away, I—"

Then the owner of the voice came rushing over the peak.

Oliver found himself face to face with a boy dressed in a familiar flying outfit, with fur-lined boots and leather gloves and a wool cap exactly like the ones Oliver was wearing.

"Who are you?" gasped Oliver.

Last night, looking into this boy's face had been like looking into a mirror. But in the daylight, the face was not quite identical. The other boy looked somewhat gaunt, with sunken eyes and a pale complexion. His left hand was wrapped in a large bandage.

The sunken eyes widened with delight. "Hullo, Oliver!" the boy said with a smile and a cough.

7

"You kidnapped Great-uncle Gilbert," said Oliver, stunned, advancing on the boy.

"Yes!" said the other boy, stumbling back. "I mean, no!"

"Who are you?" said Oliver again. "Are you my twin? What are those things chasing my kite?"

"No, no, I'm not your twin," the other boy said desperately. His smile had been replaced by wide-eyed fright as Oliver came closer. He coughed again. "The crimson kite will be fine—don't worry. The hunters are just going to capture it, that's all. It won't be hurt!" He held out his kite like a shield.

Oliver glanced at the kite—a beautiful green-and-black power kite he could not help admiring—then snapped back to the other boy. "Hunters? Those fighting kites? Who were you talking to?"

Now the other boy looked terrified. "Why don't you come back to the treehouse with me? Great-uncle Gilbert can explain everything!"

Oliver stopped short. "Great-uncle Gilbert? He's back?" That had been a very brief kidnapping.

"Y-yes. He's fine," said the other boy. "Please, just come with me."

The other boy was lying. Oliver could see it instantly. The way his eyes shifted and his voice pitched unnaturally high. Oliver wondered if he himself looked this obvious when he told lies. He remembered involuntarily a couple of the worst lies he had told, and cringed.

Then he noticed the other boy's handvane. The instrument had the usual vanes showing the wind's direction and speed, but it also had a flat, shiny surface on which glowed some large numerals. Oliver had never seen anything like it.

"What kind of handvane is that?" he asked, pointing.

"Oh, this?" said the other boy. He looked at his wrist. "It's just a regular handvane."

"I've never seen a handvane like that," said Oliver accusingly.

"Oh, right!" said the other boy. "Well, it's partly a watch, also."

"A watch?"

"It tells time," the other boy said evasively. "You'll know everything soon, from Great-uncle Gilbert." He hurried past Oliver, who followed right behind, wondering how a handvane could tell time. In Windblowne, water clocks at the bottom of the mountain kept the time and rang out hourly to be heard all over the mountain. Judging from the sun, Oliver thought those clocks should have rung by now, but he had not heard a single bell. And the crest was still deserted.

"Well? Have you caught it?"

Oliver jumped. It was the crackled, muffled voice, and it seemed to be coming from the other boy's handvane. "What was that?" Oliver asked.

The other boy touched something on his handvane, and the crackling noise stopped. "I told you, Great-uncle Gilbert will explain everything," he said over his shoulder.

"You're lying!" said Oliver.

But the other boy did not reply. Instead, in a smooth and perfect motion, he tossed his power kite into the air and leapt. He soared expertly down the crest, a flawless jump, and landed near the oakline. Oliver fell to his knees as he watched the boy tumble upon landing, then pick himself up and scurry, limping, down the formerly secret path. This was a heartbreaking sight, because this twin, even when sick, was obviously a jumper of great skill and, judging from his kite, an expert kitesmith, too.

Oliver stood and raced down the crest, down the formerly secret path, which now appeared to be immaculately groomed all the way to Great-uncle Gilbert's treehouse—

Oliver stopped, shocked, as the treehouse came into view.

Not only had the secret path somehow been cleared out during the night, but Great-uncle Gilbert's treehouse had been completely rebuilt. Whereas before his home had been carefully camouflaged so that you could not find it unless you were standing right in front of it, this new treehouse revealed itself proudly, glinting and flashing in the sunlight. Where the treehouse had once sagged, it was now flat, and where it had veered off at odd angles, it was now straight. It loomed larger and taller. The new treehouse looked as though it were made mostly of metal, something Oliver had never imagined was possible.

In fact, this entire treehouse was the product of skills and materials stranger than anything Oliver had ever seen.

The front door slid open smoothly. A figure strode out—Great-uncle Gilbert.

But it wasn't Great-uncle Gilbert, Oliver realized. Yes, this man had the same wild hair, and the same piercing blue eyes, and something like the same face. But unlike Great-uncle Gilbert, this man was wiry and trim, and instead of a robe, he wore a strange-looking outfit tailored to fit his body closely, all white with long sleeves and pants, and shiny shoes.

Another difference between this man and Great-uncle Gilbert was that he seemed deliriously happy to see Oliver. His face wore an expression of immense pleasure, with a smile that lit his face from ear to ear, revealing a perfect set of completely white teeth. He had his hands in his pockets and was rocking back and forth on his heels excitedly.

The other boy, who was standing at the foot of the steps, spoke. "I've caught—I mean, I've brought him, Great-uncle Gilbert."

"Now, now," admonished the man severely. "You are to use my new title at all times."

The other boy swallowed hard. "I'm sorry, Gr—I mean, Lord Gilbert," he said shakily.

Lord Gilbert nodded, satisfied, then fixed his attention on Oliver. "Welcome, Oliver, welcome!" he proclaimed happily. "Welcome to your new home!"

8

"My new home?" said Oliver.

"My new home?" said the other boy.

Lord Gilbert frowned. "This could get confusing." He pointed at Oliver. "You shall be known as One." He pointed at the other boy. "And you shall be Two!"

"Why am I Two?" said the other Oliver, looking wounded. "I was here first."

"You failed in a crucial assignment," sniffed Lord Gilbert. "You've been demoted."

Oliver, utterly dumbstruck, did not participate in this argument. He gaped at all of the metal piled up in that smooth, shining treehouse. And then to the side there were enormous gates—more metal!—from behind which a metallic shaft emerged and rose straight up, tall as an oak. All of the black strings from the giant oaks twisted into this shaft and wove down through it until they disappeared behind the gates. Whatever was behind the gates hummed and throbbed. Oliver could feel it vibrating in the ground and smelled a putrid odor.

Then came wind, blowing rattling leaves around his feet, and then the persistent headache that had plagued him since he had landed stabbed back, now many times worse. The world spun, and Oliver cried out, staggering, holding his head in his hands.

"Goodness!" cried Lord Gilbert. "Oliver One is unwell. Take him inside, Two, and put some breakfast in him. The trauma of his arrival has overwhelmed his primitive brain!"

Two hurried Oliver inside. Lord Gilbert strode behind. The front door opened for them with a faint *whir*. Oliver stumbled, the pain in his head leaving him unable to resist. The pain stopped abruptly when the door *whirred* shut behind them, sealing them off from the outdoors. Oliver found himself in the kitchen. He blinked stupidly.

The whole room was filled with bright light, but there was not a lamp or a window to be seen. Instead, light glared from flat panels in the ceiling. A low, whining hum came from all directions. In his great-uncle's treehouse, this room would be the kitchen, and there would be a woodstove, an icebox, and other comforts. But here, everything seemed to be made of cold, shining metal, with polished and curved surfaces, or else a kind of white surface resembling candle wax that had been melted and shaped. But it had to be the kitchen, as there were some gray cubes frying on a counter—without a fire!—and though Oliver was not sure what the cubes were supposed to be, they did have a baconish smell. Oliver's stomach rumbled.

While he stood there, rumbling and dumbstruck, Lord Gilbert began to pace, babbling gleefully. "I, of course, am Lord Gilbert, though you may refer to me simply as 'Lord,' if you wish. Although," he said, tapping a finger against his chin, "perhaps you could call *me* 'Lord Great-uncle,' as I shall be more family to you than *he* ever was. No, that sounds absurd. 'Lord Gilbert' will do."

"What?" said Oliver, trying to gather his wits. He realized that he was still blinking stupidly and tried to make himself stop.

"For example, I intend to provide you with a new kite

to replace your old one," Lord Gilbert continued, rubbing his hands together. "Two here has many kites. You can have your pick! Two won't object, will you, Two?"

"No, sir," whispered Two. He stood with his head bowed, shivering, staring at the floor.

"And though it is quite unexpected, I am simply delighted to have you here!" Lord Gilbert grinned in evident pleasure. "Two has been very useful to me—very useful!—and now your efforts will be doubled!"

This snapped Oliver back to his senses. "My efforts? What's going on? Where's my great-uncle? What's happened to his treehouse?" he demanded. He had intended that to sound tough and confident, but it emerged rather squeakily. Lord Gilbert's beaming smile was making him nervous. Everything in this shining, polished kitchen had thrown him off balance.

"Oliver One," Lord Gilbert said conversationally, "it occurs to me that you have absolutely no understanding of your current situation. *He* never bothered to explain anything to you, did he?"

Oliver simmered. He understood *he* to refer to Great-uncle Gilbert. He was humiliated to admit that his great-uncle had indeed never explained all of these twins and metal treehouses, or anything else at all, for that matter.

"Sit down," instructed Lord Gilbert with a superior grin, "and *I'll* explain everything."

Oliver sat reluctantly.

Lord Gilbert sat down as well. He laced his fingers together and sucked in a deep breath, then exhaled. He fixed his eyes on Oliver. "I will attempt to explain this in terms that a primitive person from a backward world would understand—"

"Primitive?" interrupted Oliver. "I—"

"Silence!" commanded Lord Gilbert. "I am simply concerned about your mental well-being. Giving you the truth all at once could short-circuit your delicate mental—"

"It will not short-circuit anything," said Oliver. He did not know what *short-circuit* meant, and he wasn't about to admit it.

"Very well," sighed Lord Gilbert. "You are lucky, boy. You have traveled from one Windblowne—an unsophisticated, backward place—to another Windblowne— an advanced, forward-thinking place. A different world entirely."

Oliver was surprised. Or rather, he expected to feel surprised. But he remembered Great-uncle Gilbert asking him if he were Oliver from *this* mountain, and he remembered his great-uncle's scrawled poem: *whisper to me, of oaks which dwell across the worlds.* And he remembered landing here and how the colors and scents and especially the sound of the winds had not been quite right.

Lord Gilbert got up and paced, lecturing. "Travel between these worlds is possible, of course——"

"Another world," whispered Oliver. "Great-uncle Gilbert discovered how to travel to another world!"

A pained expression came over Lord Gilbert's face. "Yes, months ago, with a sort of beginner's luck, *he* accidentally stumbled upon the secret, though I'd seen hints of it years before that. Naturally, it is up to me to perfect the process, to mechanize and maximize it! I've nearly mastered it with my own machine——"

"Nearly?" said Oliver.

Lord Gilbert grimaced. "There are still certain—— *imperfections*——in my machine. The process *damages* the subject in transit——"

"Damages?"

Lord Gilbert cleared his throat. "My experiments have

revealed that the traveler, shall we say, gradually sickens as a result of the transfers. The more trips, the more damage. Eventually, he dies. This is rather inefficient, of course. Somehow *he*—"

"They sicken and die?" said Oliver, shocked. "But I feel fine!"

"Yes," replied Lord Gilbert sourly. "Don't interrupt. It seems that in his primitive way, *he* had a kind of native cleverness, and *he* was able to construct one of these *kites*"—he spat the word with derision—"in such a way that it could carry someone—only someone small, such as a child—across the Way Between Worlds and between Windblownes, without harming the passenger."

Carry a child between Windblownes. Oliver glared at Two.

"But of course, more capacity is needed!" said Lord Gilbert. "I need to be able to stride through all the worlds myself, spreading my wisdom everywhere! Backward worlds like yours shall be modernized by my inventions! Think of it, boy! I'll need to move people— whole towns! I'll need to move machines, so that—"

"All the worlds?" Oliver said, surprised. "You mean there's more than just two?"

Lord Gilbert gave him a pitying look, shaking his

head. "Primitive boy. Yes, there are far more than two, and you should ask yourself why your great-uncle never told you about any of this. He probably did not trust you, nor think you capable of grasping this concept."

"That's not true!" said Oliver hotly.

Lord Gilbert smirked. "Perhaps," he said. "But it is something for you to think about, isn't it? Which of us trusted you with the truth?"

Oliver could not answer. Two was looking at him now, with those hollow, sunken eyes. "What did you do to Great-uncle Gilbert?" Oliver snarled at the other boy.

"Now, now," Lord Gilbert continued. "Two is hardly responsible for the capture of my idiot twin."

Oliver bristled at this description. Great-uncle Gilbert might be a number of things, but he was no idiot. "But I saw him. My great-uncle was fighting those hunters." *And if I hadn't distracted him,* Oliver remembered, *he might have won.*

"Yes," said Lord Gilbert. He strolled to the counter and spooned up some of the baconish cubes. "But the plan was mine. Unfortunately, Two failed miserably at maintaining the element of surprise, and as a result failed miserably at his secondary objective. An objective that you have managed to accomplish for me." He tossed the plate onto the table with a clatter. "Have some breakfast."

"No," said Oliver. "I want my great-uncle."

"Don't be uncooperative," said Lord Gilbert severely. "Your great-uncle was uncooperative. He would not explain the workings of his device, so I banished him to a hell-world, the most loathsome and horrible of the worlds I have discovered so far." He pushed the plate closer to Oliver. "Eat."

A hell-world? Oliver's blood began to pound. "No," he said, crossing his arms. "I want my great-uncle and I want my kite."

"Ah, the kite," Lord Gilbert continued, clapping his hands together. "I am looking forward to examining it. After last night's debacle, I wasn't sure I'd ever see it again. Fortunately, you've brought it straight to me."

"No, I haven't," said Oliver.

"Yes," replied Lord Gilbert, "you have." He reached into a cabinet and brought forth a cylinder, which to Oliver looked like a handvane without the vane. The thing was made of metal, like so many things in this world, and was covered with buttons and dials. Lord Gilbert snapped the cylinder onto his wrist, and a number of blinking lights appeared on its surface. With a giggle, he pushed some of the buttons in rapid succession.

"What is that thing?" asked Oliver.

"This," proclaimed Lord Gilbert, "is one of my most clever and useful inventions. I call it the Handvane Mark IV—HM IV for short!"

Oliver was unimpressed. "What good is a handvane without any vanes? You can't read the wind."

Lord Gilbert rolled his eyes. "An utter waste of time. The HM IV can do far more interesting things."

"Doesn't look like it's doing much right now," Oliver observed.

"Just you wait, Oliver One." Lord Gilbert smirked. The lights on the HM IV, which had been blinking randomly, began flashing on and off in unison. "This is just one of the wonders you'll discover, my boy, living here under my command!"

"That sounds great," said Oliver, standing. He edged toward the door. "I'll just need to get my kite and fly home and get a few of my things."

With a surprisingly agile leap, Lord Gilbert was in front of him, blocking his way. "Oh no, Oliver One . . .

you can't go home again, ever. You are far too useful to me. I've long needed another assistant of Two's caliber, and now I have one!"

"I'm leaving," announced Oliver. He moved to push past Lord Gilbert.

"Sit down," said Lord Gilbert.

"No."

"Sit!" commanded Lord Gilbert.

Oliver sat.

Or, more precisely, he fell, and Lord Gilbert slid a chair underneath him on the way down. Oliver's entire body had gone numb. He tried to move, but nothing below his neck would respond. He looked at Lord Gilbert, who gave him a wink. Oliver saw that he was twisting a dial on the HM IV.

"Don't despair, my boy," Lord Gilbert said, resuming his mad pacing. "You wouldn't have gotten far anyway. My beautiful and deadly hunters would have seen to that! As they will see to your crimson kite. Then the dissection can begin."

"Dissection?" said Oliver, straining to move his arm.

"Ah yes," said Lord Gilbert. "You wouldn't know about such things. But you'll learn! A dissection involves slicing up the device into its constituent components, so that I can learn how it performs the transport without damaging its cargo."

Oliver glared at Two. "Liar! You said it wouldn't be hurt! You—"

"I didn't know!" protested Two. "I thought—"

"Olivers!" shouted Lord Gilbert. "Rule one in this house is that there is to be no fighting! Oliver One, you really must learn some manners. Manners are one of the first things I was forced to teach young Two here, after his parents' disappearance."

His parents' disappearance? Oliver struggled futilely to move his legs. "I want the kite and I want my great-uncle!"

"Your one-track mind, my boy," said Lord Gilbert severely, "is becoming quite irritating. I see that I shall have to teach you some manners as well, now that you are living here with me."

"I'm not living with you," said Oliver, glaring. "I'm taking the kite and finding my great-uncle and going home."

Lord Gilbert licked his lips. "Oh, you will live with me indeed. You shall assist me with my experiments. And you shall make me many more hunters."

Oliver was stunned. "You want *me* to make them?"

"Of course!" snapped Lord Gilbert. "Using your extraordinary kitesmithing talents, the same as Two. I provide the brains and he provides the kite! I need more hunters, many more, and with two of you I can double the output!"

Oliver was just opening his mouth to tell the bitter truth about his kitesmithing skills when the HM IV suddenly emitted a loud, birdlike chirp. Lord Gilbert grinned. "Ah, my creations have returned." He twisted the dial on the HM IV, and Oliver sensed feeling returning to his arms and legs. He stood immediately.

"Now don't get any ideas, Oliver One," warned Lord Gilbert. He waved the HM IV threateningly. "Let's go see my hunters." He gestured, and Oliver went grudgingly onto the balcony at the top of the steps. Lord Gilbert followed.

Oliver stepped outside into a blustery, late-morning wind. Instantly, his piercing headache returned. He closed his eyes, wincing.

"Something wrong?" asked Lord Gilbert idly, coming alongside.

Not wanting to show any weakness, Oliver took his

hands from his head, formulating a sarcastic reply. He opened his mouth to deliver it—

and opened his eyes—

In all the history of Windblowne, going back 455 years, the giant oaks had always stood unyielding. They gave the people of Windblowne homes and protection. No one in Windblowne could ever consider harming an oak.

Or so Oliver had thought.

If you had asked him what the most terrible, horrible thing you could possibly do to an oak would be, Oliver might have said, with a shudder, "Cut it down."

Now Oliver saw there was a far worse fate, and it was the fate of the great oak nearest Lord Gilbert's treehouse.

For Lord Gilbert had touched another button on the HM IV, and the big metal gates next to the treehouse had slid smoothly aside, revealing an oak, or what was left of one.

The oak had been stripped of its branches and split down its center. The two broken halves leaned out to either side, where they sagged against supporting struts made of metal. Tubes running into the tree seemed to be collecting sap, and the oak was scorched and burned in many places. It was pierced by spikes covered with blinking lights. Surrounding all of this was a mass of cables, spilling from the base of the tall metal shaft and spiraling around the oak before twisting into openings connected to humming machines. Amid the jumble of machines was a large, mirror-like disc, the place at which all of the tubes from the mutilated oak converged. The oak was ripped and gutted and torn and broken. The ground around the tree, however, was well-tended, and another machine was carefully applying water around the roots.

Horror-struck, Oliver realized the oak was still alive.

"I see you're admiring my project," said Lord Gilbert proudly. "Isn't it marvelous? All those little machines working as one." He glanced at the sky. "Ah, my hunters have returned. And they've brought me a present!"

Oliver, glad to look at anything besides the tortured oak, looked up. Seven dark dots, arcing and weaving, had appeared against the sky.

Lord Gilbert went on. "A kite, Oliver One, can be more than a silly toy made from bamboo and silk. It can also be a beautiful, deadly predator, a hunter of the sky, made much more dangerous by my brilliant—" He broke off, frowning and flicking buttons on the HM IV. "Why haven't they got it yet?"

The dark dots drew closer. Oliver could see that one of them was the crimson kite, darting about, trying to break free from the orb of hunters that surrounded it. At each dart, one of the hunters flew swiftly to intercept. With each of these maneuvers, the kite was forced closer to the treehouse. In seconds they were directly overhead.

Lord Gilbert muttered angrily and jabbed a button on the HM IV, and the shrieking hunters collapsed upon the kite.

Oliver cried out as the crimson kite burst free in a desperate dive.

One hunter, wings folded, dove after it.

The kite streaked directly at the machine, threading a harrowing path through the wires, the hunter only inches behind. At the last moment, the crimson kite pitched upward. Unable to react, the hunter slammed into the mirror disc with a thunderous crack. Blinking lights went wild as sparks and smoke exploded from the machines around the oak. The hunter ricocheted off the disc, banged into the metal treehouse wall, and collapsed onto the balcony.

Lord Gilbert howled and raced to the balcony railing.

Oliver found himself at the top of the steps, shouting. For a moment he thought the crimson kite might be able to fly to him, and they could somehow escape. But the remaining five hunters had taken a tactically commanding position above the disc. The crimson kite flew straight into them and was attacked immediately. Then all of them were obscured by the smoke pouring from below.

Oliver whirled toward the damaged hunter, which was writhing and jerking on the balcony floor.

Oliver had never seen anything like this kite. It had the trim frame and bowed spars of a fighter but the shape of a hawk, with an array of metal spars forming a skeletal head and body. Knifelike talons protruded from the ends of what would be its legs. The sails were made of something, not silk, that Oliver didn't recognize. One of its wings flicked up, and Oliver saw gears and spokes, meshing and grinding as the hunter struggled on the balcony. It flipped itself onto its back, and beneath the head Oliver spotted a metal box with a kind of screen that emitted horrid sounds—buzzes and whirs and hisses and shrieks like nothing Oliver had ever heard before.

And then something on the metal box clicked open. A glass eye.

Oliver stumbled backward, frightened, as the thing jerked about, shrieking, metal talons scrabbling on the balcony.

The flock of hunters flew out of the smoke. Four of them glided gracefully to the balcony railing. The last circled just overhead, screeching triumphantly. Oliver saw the crimson kite twitching helplessly, clenched in metal talons.

Lord Gilbert glared at Oliver. "Well," he said, his voice tight with anger, "it seems your friend put up quite a fight." He touched a button on the HM IV, which gave a whistle, and held out his arms.

The hunter swooped in toward the balcony and released its quarry. The kite fell into Lord Gilbert's hands.

Lord Gilbert's face was filled with fury. Oliver looked at the kite and cried out. It had been terribly hurt. Half its tail was torn away, and there were two long slashes in its sails. Lord Gilbert clenched it in quivering hands that had turned bloodless white. The kite trembled painfully, ripped and wounded and helpless.

Then Lord Gilbert's look of fury vanished, and his face went suddenly, terribly, cold. "You," he said grimly, "you'll never escape from me again."

And then, with one swift and devastating move, he grasped the spine of the crimson kite and snapped it in half. The crack echoed through the silent forest. The kite's trembling ceased. Lord Gilbert threw the shattered spar to one side, then hurled the kite to the floor, where it lay crumpled and still.

Oliver screamed and lunged at Lord Gilbert.

9

Oliver reached for Lord Gilbert's throat.

Halfway through the lunge, he froze and crashed to the balcony deck. He found himself looking at one of Lord Gilbert's exquisitely polished shoes, unable to move a muscle. The shoe reached out and tucked itself under his shoulder, then flipped him onto his back.

He stared up at Lord Gilbert, whose smirking face was framed by the branches of his oak tree. "Naughty, naughty," said Lord Gilbert, lifting a finger from the HM IV and wagging it at Oliver. "Mustn't attack your legal guardian—rule number two." Whistling, he retrieved the crimson kite from where it lay in a crumpled heap. He spread it on the railing and examined it. He seemed cheerful again after his brief bout of fury.

Out of one corner of his eye, Oliver could see the wounded hunter, still sputtering and sparking on the balcony floor.

"Prop him up against the wall. I don't like him lying there," Lord Gilbert said. Two's face came into view. Oliver felt hands under his shoulders. He was dragged to a wall and propped awkwardly against it. Two would not meet his eyes.

Two crept over to the injured hunter and knelt beside it, stroking it gently as it lay writhing on the deck. A breeze blew over them all, bringing a swirl of dead oak leaves that pattered against Oliver's skin. His skull buzzed with pain.

He fought to speak, but this time he could not even move his jaw.

"Hmmm," muttered Lord Gilbert as he handled the crimson kite. "Perhaps that was a bit hasty."

"You didn't have to do that," said Two, sounding upset. He was cradling the hunter in his hands. "You didn't have to kill the kite."

"It damaged my beautiful machine," said Lord Gilbert calmly. "Punishment was required." He shot a wink in Oliver's direction.

He crumpled the kite in his fist and gathered the broken pieces of spine. Then he strode to the edge of the balcony and surveyed his machine.

"A broken hunter was just what we needed," he said over his shoulder to Two. "Oliver One can begin his training by learning how to fix it. Take it inside for now, and fetch my helmet. I have to repair the machine. And you," he said to Oliver, "you may get up, once your ability to move returns. But my hunters are watching, so resist thoughts of mischief, unless you'd like a nice scratch."

Oliver lay against the wall, bursting with rage and despair. There was also a terrific itch on his left leg that he was trying to ignore. The hunters were lined up together on the balcony rail, perfectly unmoving. Oliver could see their eyes, made of dead, black glass, staring out fixedly at nothing.

Across the balcony, Two was murmuring to the hunter. His face was twisted with its own rage and despair.

Then the other boy rose, cradling the hunter gingerly, and walked past Oliver into the treehouse. He muttered as he passed, his voice trembling, "It's not their fault they're like this. He forces them to obey him."

Oliver lay motionless, not sure if he ever really wanted to move again.

Lord Gilbert, swinging the remains of the crimson kite and whistling happily, strolled along the line of hunters. "Beautiful, are they not?" he said to Oliver. "I suppose they must seem like magic to your primitive mind."

Oliver struggled to work his tongue, but the most he could manage was a strangled moan.

Lord Gilbert frowned. "What's that, boy? You want to know more about my hunters? Of course! They are magnificent creations, much superior to your great-uncle's primitive kites, as you have seen." He grasped the nearest hunter by its wing. "Wings made of a synthetic fiber I developed, far tougher than silk! Watch!" He pinched the wing hard and pulled. The hunter shrieked and struggled. "Can't be torn!" gasped Lord Gilbert, pressing a button on the HM IV. The hunter quieted.

He moved to the next kite and ran his finger along one of the metal spars that formed the hunter's wing. "This alloy, also my invention, is lighter and stronger than steel."

"Mlp!" gulped Oliver. It looked to him like the hunter shuddered at Lord Gilbert's touch.

"And, of course, the brain," said Lord Gilbert, touching the next hunter between its eyes. "My second-proudest creation." He stroked the hunter's head, just above the blank, glassy eyes. "I take the brain straight from the living hawk, with its predatory intelligence completely intact. The perfect hunter."

Oliver would have shivered, if he could.

"I conceived of the hunters while watching Two waste his time with those ludicrous bamboo kites. I knew his talents could be put to far better use. And so they have, and so yours will as well!"

Oliver would have laughed. Lord Gilbert was going to be very disappointed with his talents.

There was a loud bang, and lights on the machine began flashing. "Two!" shouted Lord Gilbert.

Two reappeared. "Your helmet, sir."

Lord Gilbert jammed the helmet onto his head. The thing included a big pair of protective goggles and several thin metal spines pointing straight up. He looked perfectly ridiculous, and perfectly pleased with himself, as he strutted to his machine and opened a flashing-light panel next to the mirror disc. He soon had his arms deep within, working, and he barked orders to Two, who scurried about with a screwdriver, obeying.

"I need to run a test," announced Lord Gilbert after a few minutes. "Get onto the disc, boy."

"What?" said Two in disbelief. "I can't!"

"What?" said Lord Gilbert. "Why not?"

"I'm—" Two coughed. "I'm—"

"You're what?" snapped Lord Gilbert impatiently. "Sick? You're not sick, you're just weak. You can easily make several more trips before you expire. My machine is nearly perfect! Get onto the disc."

Two's eyes flashed to Oliver's, who looked away. There was nothing he could do, even if he wanted to, though a tingling feeling was covering his scalp, and he felt he might be able to move his neck.

"Now!" ordered Lord Gilbert.

Two limped reluctantly toward the riven oak, stepping onto the mirror disc.

Lord Gilbert jabbed a button on the HM IV.

A blinding flash of light.

A deafening *BANG*.

Oliver's ferocious headache surged, and he shut his eyes against the pain. When it faded, he opened his eyes. His view was obscured by a rustling cascade of dead oak leaves showering down. When the leaves cleared, he looked at the disc.

Two had vanished.

Lord Gilbert seemed unconcerned, coolly manipulating controls and whistling his jaunty whistle.

Then, with a flourish, Lord Gilbert reached out and twisted a large knob. There was another *FLASH* and another *BANG,* and when Oliver opened his eyes and another cascade of leaves had fallen past, he saw that Two was standing on the disc once more.

Standing—but not for long. The boy swayed, leaning against a railing at the back of the disc, then collapsed onto his knees, clutching his stomach.

"Well?" shouted Lord Gilbert tensely, pulling off his goggles.

Two shook his head and muttered something that Oliver could not hear.

Lord Gilbert pounded a fist on the flashing panel, then went back to fiddling with knobs as Two rolled onto his back in what looked to be terrible agony.

Oliver craned his neck. The leaf cover was evaporating with each flash and bang. The autumn oaks were becoming winter oaks, rapidly, and not from the gentle, natural fall of the seasons but from the ruthless, artificial violation of Lord Gilbert's machines. The sinister black strings and sap-filled tubes and metal spikes—these were what was causing the oak leaves to fall.

A few more leaves stirred from their branches as a puff of wind blew over the platform. Oliver watched them tumble past. The leaves were identical to those of the sick oak outside Great-uncle Gilbert's treehouse, and with them came a disgusting scent—a sour odor—where had he smelled it before? Oliver took a deep sniff. . . .

And then he knew.

Like the ticking gears of a Windblowne water clock, pieces of the puzzle fell into place.

tick—He had indeed smelled this odor before—outside Great-uncle Gilbert's treehouse. The smell from the sick oak. Looking down from the balcony, Oliver could see that the sick oak at Great-uncle Gilbert's treehouse was in the exact same location as the riven oak here.

His great-uncle's notes:

"the winds do not whisper . . .
but if you do whisper, O winds, then
whisper to me,
of oaks which dwell across the worlds."

Oaks which dwell across the worlds. The sick oak there, the riven oak here—they had the same leaves. They were the same tree.

tick—Oaks on the mountain, losing their leaves in both Windblownes.

Oliver remembered his arrival in this Windblowne, how he had known right away that something was different about the world. The colors, the scents, the sounds, everything had been subtly altered. The only thing that had seemed the same to him was the oak leaves. Somehow, the oaks *were* the same—they lived in both worlds. And the damage from Lord Gilbert's machines and those black strings was affecting Oliver's Windblowne as well.

tick—

A crimson kite made from oak. A kite that traveled between worlds. The secret to traveling between worlds lay in the oaks.

Feeling returned to Oliver's body, and he was able to stand. He looked warily at Lord Gilbert's hunters. They perched silently in a row, not looking at Oliver, not looking at anything.

He started toward the steps. A cold fury filled him. He would finish the work the crimson kite started. He would smash the machines that were torturing the oak. He'd find a weapon—anything—and hammer them to pieces and pull down the black strings. He was not sure if there was still time to save the tree. But he would do as much damage as possible before Lord Gilbert could stop him.

He had taken only three steps when the nearest hunter raised a metal talon, lowered its *synthetic fiber* wings, and, looking directly at Oliver with its cold, glassy eyes, gave a menacing croak.

Oliver stood motionless. One by one, the other hunters turned their heads and fastened their empty stares upon him.

He took a step back, carefully, then another. The hunters' gazes did not waver. Not until he felt the tree-house wall behind him did he realize he had been holding his breath.

Oliver heard a chuckle. Lord Gilbert was watching him with amusement. "You see, One," he said, "things can go very badly for you if you don't cooperate." He gave his flashing panel a loving stroke. "My machine is all better. Now your training can begin. Two will teach you everything you need to know about the hunters. I'm sure it will seem intimidating at first, but have no fear. Your natural engineering talents will shine through. Join us in my laboratory!"

Lord Gilbert rushed past Oliver, snatching up the remains of the crimson kite. He continued inside. Two limped up the steps after him.

Oliver, looking at the row of hunters, realized that he had no choice but to follow, for now.

He heard voices from the direction of the workshop, or what Lord Gilbert had called his *laboratory*. He stalked to the doorway.

Right away, Oliver could see that a laboratory was like a workshop, except that all of the normal tools were replaced with more devices that blinked and hummed. There were workbenches made out of that smooth whitish stuff, and long tables, and racks of inscrutable equipment.

And there were fifty-six more hunters.

Oliver knew there were exactly fifty-six, because there were rows of narrow hutches built into all four walls, and each one had a small plate with a number from one to one hundred. In each hutch was a hunter, folded nearly flat. Only the first fifty-six were occupied.

Oliver stopped in the doorway.

"Don't be afraid," said Two. "None of these are activated." He was hunched down on a stool, shivering.

"I'm not afraid," said Oliver. He stepped into the laboratory and leapt a foot into the air as he heard a scrabbling sound beside him.

The noise came from one of several birdcages hanging in a corner. In the cage crouched a small, quivering hawk with wide, frightened eyes. It was pressed as far as possible from the human occupants of the laboratory.

Next to Two was the injured hunter. He had laid it on a workbench, with its broken wing sticking straight up. It had stopped writhing and jerking. Beside the hunter lay a number of screwdrivers, wrenches, and a few other tools Oliver didn't recognize.

Lord Gilbert was bent over a kind of tablet on which the crimson kite had been stretched, its sails fixed in place by pegs. He was peering at it through a metal tube and muttering loudly, "Nothing . . . nothing!"

Oliver's eye was caught by a flash of bright blue-green. It was one of Great-uncle Gilbert's kites, folded flat on top of a stack of other colorful kites. *All of his best kites,* Oliver thought despairingly. Two had taken them all. They must have hoped that one of the others could do what the crimson kite did.

Lord Gilbert looked up from his tube and noticed Oliver. "You!" he said crossly. "Tell me more about this kite. My microscope reveals no unusual features. The sails are made of silk and the spars of ordinary oak. Where did he hide the circuitry?"

"Circuitry?" said Oliver, irritated. "I have no idea what you're talking about." Actually, Oliver did know of one unusual feature of the kite's design—the oaken spars—but he wasn't about to share that with Lord Gilbert.

Lord Gilbert looked him up and down and sighed. "No, you probably don't."

"And even if I did," Oliver continued, "I'd never tell you. I'm not going to help you, ever. I'm not like *him.*" He cast a withering glare at Two, who ducked his head. "And what's more—"

"Oh, do shut up," said Lord Gilbert. "Having two of you around is twice as annoying." He shoved the microscope aside. "A shame I couldn't force an explanation from the old fool before I banished him to that hellworld. Doubtless a few weeks of suffering will persuade him. . . ." His eyes fell on Oliver's arm. "Ah!" he said brightly. "More of *his* craftsmanship!"

"Hey!" said Oliver, backing away. But Lord Gilbert yanked Great-uncle Gilbert's beautiful handvane from Oliver's forearm, wrenching his wrist in the process. He held up his prize, turning it about, squinting and muttering.

"That's mine," Oliver lied. "I made it, so hands off!"

Lord Gilbert shrugged. "Useless." He tossed it aside on a bench and went back to digging around in Oliver's pack. Oliver reached out carefully and took the handvane, slipping it onto his wrist. Then he went to the crimson kite, where it lay pinned under the microscope, and reached for it, too.

"Don't touch," Lord Gilbert warned without looking at Oliver. He gave the HM IV a meaningful tap.

Oliver looked longingly at the kite, a terrible sadness falling over him. It was hard to believe that this poor, ragged, torn thing had ever flown at all. It looked like nothing more than an old piece of silk drooping over the edge of the workbench.

"Try to focus on the future, Oliver One," said Lord Gilbert. "This is all for the greater good. My machine, once perfected, will be able to send more than just one child, or a few letters—it will be able to send anything and anyone across all the worlds!"

"But you're killing the oaks," Oliver pointed out. "And your grandnephew."

Lord Gilbert waved a hand dismissively. "Yes, yes, there are inefficiencies. I have to draw power from the oaks on my mountain to run my machine. Soon they'll all be dead. But there are more oaks on other worlds. I'll build conduits between those worlds and this one. The oaks are limitless."

"But you're not just killing the oaks on this mountain," said Oliver. "You're killing all the oaks on all the worlds."

"Nonsense, boy," chuckled Lord Gilbert. "Don't argue with me about things you couldn't possibly understand."

"You didn't know you were killing oaks on other worlds?" said Oliver. "Don't you know the oaks are all connected? That they're all the same oaks?"

Lord Gilbert sighed heavily. "Don't expect me to try

to explain these concepts to you. But what you describe is impossible."

Oliver looked at him in disbelief. "You don't even know how your own machine works, do you?"

"Of course I do," huffed Lord Gilbert. "Phase resonance! Principles of quantum polyality!"

"You don't know," interrupted Oliver.

"I almost do," said Lord Gilbert defensively.

"But Great-uncle Gilbert knows," said Oliver with satisfaction. "And he wouldn't tell you."

Lord Gilbert gave a thin-lipped smile. "He'll be willing to cooperate soon enough."

"He'll never cooperate with you," said Oliver evenly.

"Two said that before, as well," growled Lord Gilbert. "But look at him now."

The argument was interrupted by a muffled explosion from outside. Lord Gilbert looked at the HM IV with alarm. "You!" He pointed at Two. "Train the other one. I'm needed outside." He rushed from the laboratory.

Two and Oliver looked at each other. "Well," said Two uncomfortably. "I suppose I should show you how the hunters work."

He began repairing the damaged hunter with a

screwdriver, providing detailed explanations as he went. Oliver did not understand a word. But he nodded and said, "Ah, I see!" anyway. Now that he knew what Lord Gilbert was capable of, he didn't want the old man to discover that Oliver could be no use to him at all.

He nodded, and pretended, until he realized that Two was saying something about the brain and a thought occurred to him. "Wait," he said. "Doesn't traveling between worlds with that machine hurt the hunters, too?"

Two pursed his lips. "Yes. It hurts them. It even kills them, eventually. That's why Lord Gilbert needs constant replacements. He's trying to build a whole fleet of a hundred hunters to guard him once he's able to travel to other worlds."

Oliver looked at the folded hunters in their fifty-six hutches. "Why aren't these . . . uh . . ."

"Activated?" said Two. "He's using the oaks for power. The drain from so many hunters would kill the oaks within hours. Once he can get to other worlds, he's going to build conduits that will add their power to his machine. Then he can activate them all."

"But—" Oliver began, when suddenly Lord Gilbert's voice crackled from Two's handvane.

"Two!" ordered the scratchy voice. *"The damage is worse than I feared! The machine could explode and destroy the entire mountain. I need your assistance at once!"*

"That sounds serious," said Oliver.

"It will be fine," said Two. He looked around the laboratory, then grabbed a small metal can. "This is an oilcan. The joints on each hunter have to be oiled. Can you handle that?"

"Of course," said Oliver, irate.

"Good. Get started." Two thrust the can at Oliver and hurried from the laboratory.

The oilcan appeared to have a lever on top of it. Oliver gave it an experimental squeeze, and a squirt of black fluid shot onto the floor. Quickly, Oliver set the can on a workbench and pulled a rug over the dark stain.

He looked around the laboratory. He had no intention of helping Lord Gilbert, but he had no idea how to escape from this terrible situation without the crimson kite. He needed to come up with some kind of plan. Maybe he didn't understand the equipment in the lab, but he might find something he could use among Two's kitesmithing tools.

He went upstairs to find Two's bedroom, which he guessed would double as his workshop, just like Oliver's did.

There was no mistaking the room. Everything in it—the bed, the chest, the workbench—matched the furniture in his own room at home. But there was one large and dispiriting difference. Instead of the broken spars and misshapen sails and other kitesmithing monstrosities that had littered his bedroom at home, this room was full of beautiful kites—some on racks, some hanging from the ceiling. Oliver sighed.

He fell miserably into the chair in front of the workbench. He supposed that one of these kites belonged to him now. His gaze wandered over them. The experience was eerily like looking into a daydream. Each of the magnificent kites was exactly like one he had imagined making but had failed in every attempt to construct. He thought he ought to feel happy that he now owned one of these kites. He tried to rouse himself with the idea that he could use it in the Festival. After all, it was *as if* he had made it. But that was no good.

Two had all of the talent that Oliver lacked. "Your

talents lie elsewhere," Great-uncle Gilbert had said. *Sure,* thought Oliver. *All that means is that I don't have any talents at all.*

He looked restlessly around the room. Two had probably built all of the other things that Oliver had imagined making, too.

He thought of his attempt at a secret drawer in his workbench. He looked carefully along one side of Two's workbench. The wood appeared perfectly smooth, as though no door were there. But of course, Two had the talents that Oliver lacked. He would have built the drawer properly.

Oliver placed his fingers just where he had tried to put the hidden mechanism for opening his own drawer. And he pushed.

Click.

Triumph. With a satisfying hiss, a secret drawer slid out from the workbench. Oliver felt a moment of intense jealousy, then lifted the lid on the drawer and looked inside—

And realized he just might escape after all.

10

Oliver reached into the secret drawer. He withdrew a single oaken spar, still green and sticky and freshly cut. In the drawer remained a neat row of similar spars, all oak, whittled to various lengths. Oliver ran his fingers over their tacky surfaces. They felt as though they'd all been cut within the last few days.

He turned quickly to the kites and examined them one by one. None of them had spars of oak. No one used oak to make kite spars—no one except Great-uncle Gilbert. Yet Two had been crafting oaken spars and hiding them in a secret drawer in his workbench.

Oliver dropped onto the bed, thinking furiously. Two was a skilled kitesmith, and he must have noticed the odd oaken spars of the crimson kite right away. He must have decided to make his own kite, modeled after Great-uncle Gilbert's. For some reason, he had hidden all of this from his guardian.

Oliver didn't know why, but he did know this—whatever Two was scheming, it was not going to happen. Oliver had a much better plan for these oaken spars: he would use them himself, to repair the crimson kite, and escape from this Windblowne.

He wanted to try the repair right away, but he had to wait for night, when Lord Gilbert and Two would be sleeping. So, with impatient reluctance, he replaced the sticky spars exactly as he found them, closed the secret door with a snap, and lay back on the bed to formulate every detail of his new plan. This time, he vowed, no mistakes, nothing left to chance, and no improvising. This plan had to work, absolutely, with no excuses. . . .

Oliver woke to the sound of footsteps downstairs. He sat up in a rush. He must have fallen asleep. After all, he hadn't gotten much rest last night. A delicious smell wafted into the bedroom, and Oliver realized he was famished. He was wondering if he should go downstairs and sullenly accept some lunch when he heard slow, soft steps coming up the stairs.

He buried himself under the blankets, not wanting his face to give away any hint of what he had discovered.

He heard the door open.

"I'm trying to sleep," said Oliver, his voice muffled by the bedclothes.

A weary, raspy voice replied, "Sorry."

Oliver sat up in surprise, spilling pillows. He had not recognized the voice. But it was Two, and he looked terrible. He was even thinner, as though he had lost another ten pounds in the last few hours. In his hands was a bowl, and he bent forward as he held it, as if it were a boulder.

"You don't look like you're going to make it," observed Oliver.

"Thanks," said Two. He shuffled to the workbench and placed the bowl there with trembling hands. "Here's your lunch."

"I'm not hungry," Oliver said, staring ravenously at the bowl. He was not sure what it was—some kind of complicated stew—but it looked and smelled heavenly.

He didn't think, though, that it would be a good idea to eat anything prepared by Lord Gilbert.

"It's okay," said Two, seeming to understand this. "I cooked it."

Oliver sighed. "Of course you did." Naturally, Two was also an expert chef. Oliver crawled out of bed and sat morosely at the bench. He took a bite. Yes, sadly, the stew was absolutely superb—far tastier than anything Oliver had ever managed to prepare.

Two flopped onto the bed. He stared dully at the ceiling, saying nothing.

Oliver, as he wolfed down the stew, watched him out of the corner of his eye. Two's hands would not stop shaking, and the skin on his arms and legs was raw and red. "Why are you helping Lord Gilbert?" Oliver asked between mouthfuls, trying not to sound too concerned about it. "That machine is killing you."

"I don't have any choice," said Two distantly.

"I would never work for him," mumbled Oliver with as much determination as he could muster with a mouth full of stew. He swallowed. "I would never do anything he told me to do, no matter what!"

Two fixed him with a solemn stare. "What if helping

Lord Gilbert gave you a chance to have the thing you'd always wanted most in the world?"

This gave Oliver pause. What would he do? The thing that Oliver had always wanted most in the world was to win first prize at the Festival.

"I still wouldn't do it," said Oliver. He realized with surprise that this was actually true. He had hardly given the Festival a thought all day. Oliver felt vaguely disturbed by this radical reordering of his priorities.

"You have no idea," said Two wearily.

"How do you know?" said Oliver in irritation. "What's this thing you want so badly?"

Two kept staring, saying nothing. Then, to Oliver's surprise, he asked, "What are your parents like?"

"My parents? Why would you want to know about them?"

Suddenly he remembered what Lord Gilbert had said about Two's parents' "disappearance." Of course Two would be interested in Oliver's parents.

Reluctantly, Oliver told Two about the sculptures that littered the yard, creating an eyesore and an embarrassment. He told Two about the long, boring books that almost no one read.

"They sound really nice," said Two. He had an odd and wistful expression on his face.

"Well, they're my parents." Oliver didn't know what else to say. The look on Two's face was strange and a little scary. "What happened to yours?"

Two's eyes had a faraway look. "Six years ago, Lord Gilbert began experimenting with a machine that would create free power for the whole town. He said he'd discovered unusual properties of the oaks and that he could draw energy from them without harming them."

"That's crazy," said Oliver.

Two nodded. "A lot of people thought so, but back then everyone in Windblowne loved Lord Gilbert. He's a brilliant inventor, and he'd made all kinds of devices that made life better for everyone. They were willing to let him try. I used to follow him around all the time, begging him to let me help him with his experiments. We were both inside the control booth the first time he switched on his new machine. But something went wrong. There was an enormous flash of light, and we were both knocked unconscious. When we came to, we discovered that everyone on the mountain had vanished. They were just . . . gone."

"Everyone in the entire town?" said Oliver. He remembered his mother mentioning another leaf death that had occurred six years ago.

"Yes. After that, Lord Gilbert seemed to go a little mad—"

"A little?"

"A lot," admitted Two. "He thought everyone had died. But he kept up his experiments with the machine. He convinced himself that if he could make the machine work, then the sacrifice was worth it. He had me help him wire up every oak on the mountain."

"You mean those black strings?" said Oliver.

"Wires," corrected Two.

"But what if they weren't killed?" asked Oliver, hastily covering his mistake. "What if they just got sent to another world?"

"Neither of us thought of that," said Two. "At least, not until the crimson kite arrived." Then a queasy look came over him, and he began a fit of coughing. Oliver waited impatiently. Anything he learned about this world might be something that would help him escape.

"So the crimson kite flew here," prompted Oliver.

"Yes," Two replied, recovering. "It flew in on the night

winds, carrying a letter from your great-uncle. He was searching for a reply from someone—anyone—from another Windblowne. This changed everything for Lord Gilbert. He realized his machine could transport people between worlds and had already done it once by accident."

"You should have tried to find the people from your Windblowne," advised Oliver.

Two looked annoyed. "Don't you think that was the first thing I thought of? I wanted to find my parents again. But it turned out to be impossible. What happened back then was an accident. There was no information on where everyone went, or even that they went anywhere at all. The new version of the machine tracks exactly where it sends things. Anything that travels to another world through the machine can be called back by Lord Gilbert anytime he wants. But the original machine couldn't do that. Lord Gilbert didn't seem to care anymore, though. He'd become convinced that other worlds were more primitive than ours and that they could be improved by his inventions. He thinks he's going to be the savior of all the worlds."

"But there's something Great-uncle Gilbert knows that Lord Gilbert doesn't," said Oliver, proud. "No one gets sick from traveling with the kite. And the kite doesn't need to draw energy from the oaks."

"Yes," said Two, "and that makes Lord Gilbert wild with anger. He corresponded with your great-uncle, letters flying back and forth with the crimson kite. He wanted to know how the kite worked. But your great-uncle is a little, well . . ."

"Paranoid?" said Oliver. "But he had reason to be, didn't he? The first time I met him, he accused me—I mean, accused *you*—of lying to him and betraying him."

Two looked away. He was silent for a few moments. Then: "The crimson kite offered to take me to your Windblowne. I flew to your crest and found my way to your great-uncle's treehouse—"

"I know," Oliver interrupted. "I saw your trail."

"And I saw you," said Two. "I saw you fly your kite. Well, I saw you destroy it."

Oliver gaped. "You were spying on me?"

Two looked alarmed. "Yes, but—"

"Then you know I'm no good with kites!" said Oliver. "You know I can't help you make new hunters. Why are you letting Lord Gilbert think I can? When he finds out, he'll send me to a hell-world! He'll send *you* to a hell-world!"

Two struggled to his feet. "You don't know what it's like!" he said between bouts of hacking coughs. "You don't know what it's like living here! Your great-uncle was the first friend I'd ever had!"

"Friend?" said Oliver. He jumped to his feet. "You kidnapped him and stole all his kites! You helped Lord Gilbert banish him to a hell-world! What kind of friend is that?"

But any answer Two might have given was interrupted by Lord Gilbert's voice, which erupted out of Two's handvane.

"Two! Come down immediately! We have work to do!"

The Olivers looked at each other. Two seemed on the verge of saying something, then bit his lip. "I'll explain later," he said. But Oliver could tell he was lying. Two limped from the room.

Watching him leave, Oliver wondered about the spars in the hidden drawer. Was it possible that Two intended to use them for the same thing Oliver did—to escape? If he left via kite, Lord Gilbert wouldn't be able to pull him back through the machine. He caught himself wondering what would happen to Two after Oliver took the spars—then reminded himself that Two had betrayed Great-uncle Gilbert. *He doesn't deserve my sympathy.*

Lord Gilbert's voice came again, this time out of a panel in the wall. *"Oliver One! Downstairs now!"*

Lord Gilbert, covered in soot and still wearing his helmet, was waiting for Oliver in the living room. "Well?" he barked. "The repairs will be completed shortly. Have you come to your senses? Are you ready to start with the hunters?"

"Yes, of course," said Oliver innocently. "The joints on each hunter have to be oiled. And I'm going to oil them."

"Much better," said Lord Gilbert, peering at Oliver. Then Two called something from outside, and Lord Gilbert rushed away.

Oliver had no intention of oiling the hunters. But what if Lord Gilbert checked the can? Thinking hard, Oliver went to the laboratory and removed the lid from the oilcan. Then he went into the kitchen and carefully poured the entire contents into the sink. Black liquid bubbled down the drain. Satisfied, Oliver replaced the can in the laboratory. Now Lord Gilbert would never know.

Back in the laboratory, he hunted for a ruler to get an

idea of the length of the required spine, but he couldn't find anything like one. With the inactive hunters on every side, he felt as though someone were constantly looking over his shoulder. He suspected one of the many inexplicable devices that filled the laboratory would do the job, but he had no idea which one. He searched through them all, looking for anything useful, but was afraid of raising suspicions by disturbing too much of anything when he was supposed to be oiling.

He suffered through a morose supper with Lord Gilbert and Two, who apparently had gotten the machine in working order. Lord Gilbert groused about the disruption to his schedule. Two coughed quietly. Oliver left the table as soon as he could, claiming he needed to get a lot of rest for a big day of fixing hunters tomorrow. He lay on a sofa converted to a makeshift bed in the living room, listening to a commotion from the next room as Lord Gilbert and Two dealt with some kind of kitchen catastrophe. Despite himself, he drifted off into a nervous sleep before he could find out what the catastrophe was.

He was woken by the sound of Lord Gilbert storming upstairs, growling, "First the machine, now something's wrong with the pipes! My Olivers will fix it tomorrow." Two followed soon after, limping up.

The strange lamps that filled the treehouse with light were extinguished. After waiting as long as he could bear, Oliver rose from the couch, alone downstairs in the darkened treehouse, bathed by white moonslight gleaming in through the windows. He wished it weren't the month of Two Moons. His escape would be easier under cover of total darkness.

Outside, the winds howled, sounding oddly far away, unlike in Oliver's treehouse at home, where drafts whistled in through the cracks. There were no drafts in Lord Gilbert's perfectly built treehouse.

Oliver crept into action.

11

Oliver climbed carefully, carefully, placing each foot delicately on the next step as he inched upstairs, quiet as a ghost. In his own treehouse, there would have been cacophonous creaks and groans no matter how gingerly he went. Here, in Lord Gilbert's flawless treehouse, the stairs were silent.

In the dark bedroom, Two's breathing was slow and raspy. Oliver listened for a minute, making sure Two was really asleep. *No chances, Oliver,* he warned himself. *No mistakes.*

He crawled to the workbench, thinking quiet thoughts. He felt for the mechanism that opened the secret drawer. His groping fingers found it—

CLICK!

Oliver cringed. Was that the same click as before? Had it sounded quite as much like an explosion the first time? It seemed to echo through the room—*CLICKCLICKCLICK!*

With stern orders to stop imagining things, he held his breath and reached daintily into the drawer. There was a slight clatter, and then he had all of the spars in his hand. He stole ghostly downstairs to the laboratory, tremendously pleased at how well the plan was going.

He stumbled around in the dark until his hand found a lamp. Remembering what he'd seen Lord Gilbert do, he felt for a switch and pressed it. The room flooded with soft light. *Well done,* he thought smugly. He was learning his way around this strange world.

The moment the light came on, the caged hawk in the corner began chittering fearfully. "Shhh!" Oliver hissed. He stepped back, and the hawk quieted. On a workbench near the cage was the broken hunter. The thing lay on its side, glass eyes dull and empty, one wing stuck awkwardly straight up, exposing a puzzle of wires beneath. It was no wonder the caged hawk was upset.

"I'll take you with me when I leave," Oliver whispered. "I won't let them do that to you." He thought of releasing it right away, but turning a panicked hawk loose in the laboratory seemed like a superb way to blow his cover. *No more mistakes.*

He turned his attention to the poor crimson kite, pinned to a workbench, looking discouragingly dead.

Carefully, Oliver removed the pins and clasps restraining the kite, despairing at the damage, feeling inept. Under the artificial light, the bright crimson silk looked wan and sickly. His fumbling hands seemed to cause even more damage and more rips. Tears sprang to his eyes—could the kite feel pain?

At last the kite was free. Tenderly, Oliver smoothed the silk. His heart pounded. This was where things would get tricky.

Trying not to clatter, he arranged the sticky spars on the workbench. He chose one that looked to be spine length. Taking a deep breath, he tried to fix the spar in place. Too long. He tried another. Too short. He held his breath. Would the third one be just right? No, it didn't fit either. He felt warm tears on his cheeks as he pushed and pulled, trying to fit at least one of the spars, feeling the last of his confidence draining away.

At last he found a spar that looked exactly right. Carefully, carefully, measuring with his eyes, he tried to snap it into place. But the spar was just slightly too long. Automatically, he looked around for a knife.

Then he froze. *No mistakes, Oliver.* He hated to admit it, but if he started messing about with knives or any other tools, he'd probably make things even worse.

He eyed the almost-right spar. It was so close—maybe if he just pushed a little harder, he could snap it in. After all, this kite had survived the force of the night winds— if it could do that, it could probably survive the force of his clumsiness. With a firm nod, he prepared to push.

"No!" A harsh whisper came from behind him. Oliver whirled.

Two stood holding a knife.

Oliver lunged, not thinking about the knife or the fact that he was completely unarmed.

Two threw one arm around Oliver's neck. "Quiet, you idiot!" he coughed into Oliver's ear. "You'll wake Lord Gilbert."

Oliver paused, panting, muscles tensed, wanting to fight.

Two released Oliver's neck and spoke through clenched teeth. "If you try to jam that spar in, it will snap! Give it to me."

Oliver offered it sheepishly.

Two placed the spar on the bench. Oliver watched, feeling foolish, as the boy worked rapidly, making precise measures, then in a swift slice notching a tiny cut at the end of the spar.

"Now try it," said Two calmly, returning the spar.

"Uh, better not," whispered Oliver. "You do it."

Two sighed wistfully. "No. It's your kite. You have to."

Surprised, Oliver accepted the spar. He leaned over his kite.

"Now gently," instructed Two in a low voice. "No jamming."

Gently, thought Oliver. With an echoing snap, he pressed the spine into place. A ripple flowed through the sails.

The Olivers stood riveted, watching intently.

But there was nothing else. No other ripple, not a tremble or a flutter. The crimson kite lay on the workbench, completely still.

The Olivers stood grieving and silent.

At last Two spoke, his voice plaintive. "What now?"

Oliver, devastated, tried to think. "You tell me," he whispered. "You're the kite expert!"

Two shrugged helplessly. "No, I'm not. I mean—not when it comes to this kite. I don't really understand how it works. I just tried to copy what your great-uncle did. I used spars pruned from the same oak he used, an oak next to his treehouse—"

"Of course!" said Oliver impatiently. "The sick oak. The riven oak. The same tree."

"What?"

"Oaks which dwell across the worlds," Oliver recited. "The oaks in both our worlds are connected. The riven oak in my world is dying, too."

The other boy looked alarmed. "You really meant that?"

"Yes," said Oliver. "Why?"

"If I used a spar from the riven oak," Two whispered, "then the hunters will be able to track the kite. Not its precise location, but they'll be able to narrow it down to a handful of worlds. They'll find you eventually." He looked at the crimson kite doubtfully. "Although it doesn't look like it can fly anywhere anyway."

"Maybe it only needs to feel the night winds," Oliver said. "Let's take it to the crest." He gathered the kite tenderly in his arms.

A soft *bump* came from the floor above.

Both Olivers turned and looked at the stairs leading up to Lord Gilbert's room.

"Come on!" said Two. "The wind hatch."

"Wait," said Oliver. He reached for the cage. The hawk resumed its terrible noises.

"Leave it!" said Two, grabbing Oliver's arm. "There's nothing you can do—Lord Gilbert will just send the hunters to capture it again."

"No," said Oliver, yanking free. "At least it will have a chance. And I promised."

They went into the kitchen, and Two pressed a button on the wall. The wind hatch in the floor rose silently.

Climbing proved difficult for Two in his weakened state, so Oliver descended twice, once with the cage and once with the kite. At the bottom of the lighted shaft was an enclosure, with a sliding door to the outside.

"Come on," said Two, speaking loudly now so as to be heard over the wind. He reached for the door handle but had trouble pulling it open.

"Need some help?" asked Oliver, his arms full of cage and kite.

Two coughed weakly, shivering, sweat pouring down

his brow. "No," he said. He put both hands on the door and, with a great effort, slid it open.

Outside, the night was wild and frightening. The mad, raging winds were equal to the winds of recent nights in Oliver's Windblowne, which had been the worst he'd ever seen. They almost seemed to scream at him. Oliver cried out and nearly fell.

"What's wrong?" shouted Two.

"The winds," hissed Oliver through clenched teeth. "Can't you hear it?"

"Hear what?" said Two. "Come on, we have to hurry!"

But Oliver couldn't hurry anywhere, not like this. The winds were somehow causing his headache, boring into his skull with an insistent, aching cry. He tried to focus his attention elsewhere, on the kite and his great-uncle and—

The hawk sensed open air and was battering at the sides of its cage. Oliver dropped to one knee and fumbled for the door latch, hanging on to the kite while trying not to lose a finger. At last the door popped open. There was a blur—a shriek—and the hawk was gone.

With a spinning heave, Oliver hurled the cage as far as he could into the forest, hoping that the winds would smash it to bits on an oak. "Let's go!" he said. The headache was still there, but he'd been able to push it down to a manageable level.

Together, the Olivers pushed their way through the windstorm. The winds pulled at the crimson kite, but Oliver kept it close to his body. *Not yet,* he told the winds. *Wait for the crest.*

Oliver shuddered as they passed the riven oak. The gates had been left open, and the oak's moonslit silhouette loomed over them like a beast with two arms, writhing in agony. The foul shadows of Lord Gilbert's machines hunched around, clutching at the tree. Somehow the shadows seemed hunched around Oliver, too. He hurried past, shadows on each side, peering for a way through, and then he realized Two was no longer with him.

The boy had found a pocket of calm on the leeward side of one of the machines. His whole body was shaking, and tears tumbled down his cheeks.

"Come on!" Oliver shouted.

Two shook his head, struggling to speak. Oliver leaned in close, trying to catch his words, which were faint and whispery against the wind.

". . . would have done anything for that. I'm sorry."

"Anything for what?" said Oliver.

Two seemed to be drifting away. "It's my fault—I helped him . . . but after today . . . I realized I couldn't take your family from you. . . ."

"My family?"

". . . yes . . . if I were there and you were trapped here . . ."

"That's why you helped him kidnap Great-uncle Gilbert," said Oliver suddenly. "That's why you were making a kite to escape. You wanted my family. My life. You wanted to trade places with me."

Two nodded. "I'm sorry."

Oliver stood wondering. A few days ago, the idea that someone would risk dying so that he could have Oliver's parents and Oliver's life would have seemed like the most absurd idea imaginable. But now his parents looked pretty good, compared to a great-uncle who performed scientific experiments on you, who cut the brains out of hawks, and who planned to destroy the giant oaks on one world after another. And with Two's kitesmithing talents, he'd probably be a big hero back home.

"You can still have it!" said Oliver eagerly, much to his surprise. "Sort of, anyway! We can both escape! My parents will help you!" Affection for his parents suddenly flooded him. He grasped Two's arm. "Come on! You can make it!"

"I don't think so," sighed Two, shaking his head.

"You have to!" said Oliver, tugging. "What will Lord Gilbert do when he finds out I've escaped?"

"I don't know," said Two weakly. He reached out to stroke the crimson kite. "But even if the kite can fly, could it carry two of us?"

Oliver looked down at his poor, torn kite. He didn't think it could carry even one. "I don't know," he said. "But we can at least try."

Two shook his head. "I"—he coughed—"I can't make it to the crest in these winds." He slid down the side of the machine.

"Come on!" ordered Oliver. "You can!" He fought to pull Two to his feet.

"No!" croaked Two, his eyes wide with fear.

Oliver began to argue, then realized Two was not looking at him; he was looking at something over Oliver's shoulder.

Oliver turned.

High in Lord Gilbert's treehouse, windows blazed with light.

12

"Go!" screamed Two. He pushed Oliver's hands away and struggled to sit up, hands slipping in the grass.

Oliver hesitated.

Two shouted furiously. "Go, or I'll—" He punched weakly at Oliver.

Oliver stood. "I'll come back for you! I'll find Great-uncle Gilbert and—"

But Two was crawling now, crawling back toward the treehouse, whose windows were flaring up one after another. Lord Gilbert's treehouse was waking.

Oliver took a last look at the riven oak. *I'll come back for you, too,* he promised. Then he was running as the treehouse came alive with blazing lights, sending beams stabbing through the nearly leafless oaks, illuminating their bare branches, making an eerie labyrinth of unnatural shadows. Somehow he felt that Lord Gilbert was watching him, and maybe he was, with mysterious machines like eyes glaring down. As Oliver ran, he felt more and more like a tiny mouse, escaping from a—

A hawk. Oliver realized he had completely forgotten about the hunters.

Something heavy and hard slammed into his back. A flash of pain tore across his shoulder, and he crashed to the ground. Fear flashed through him too—the crimson kite!—but the impact had knocked it away. He rolled over in agony, his breath gone, groping for his kite, but it was nowhere to be felt.

Through the haze of pain he heard a vicious *whish* as another hunter shot past. He struggled to his feet, shoulder screaming, looking around wildly for anything crimson. A chorus of screeching warnings cracked the air.

"RETURN AT ONCE!"

A booming voice—Lord Gilbert's—seemed to come from everywhere. It boomed up the mountain, drowning out even the winds, making Oliver clap his hands to his ears. Somehow Lord Gilbert could project his voice like thunder, rumbling over the oaks and into the moonslit sky.

Oliver spied a burst of crimson smashing helplessly out of control between oaks, at the mercy of the winds. He chased after it as a hunter whizzed by the edge of his vision, black and low, and pain tore through his arm. He ground his teeth to keep from screaming. He ran onward, then dove for the kite just as another hunter swooped in, talons raking. He could hear it shriek as it struck him.

He had the kite in his hands.

The oak in front of him had distinctive branches, dipping just so, as if to point the way. It was one of the sentinels. The oak next to it, the second sentinel, was also pointing. His map of the mountain clicked into place. He started toward the crest.

Out of habit, he glanced at the handvane on his wrist. It looked undamaged, but though the winds were swirling all around, the pointer did not waver. It pointed resolutely in one direction—west.

It's broken, thought Oliver. In these winds, the pointer ought to be spinning like mad.

The pain in his shoulder and back and head began to be a lesser concern than the pain in his chest. Oliver had never run like this, and he could not seem to get enough air. Blurs came down from the sky, some missing, some hitting, as though he were in a hellish hailstorm.

Still he ran, at last reaching the oakline.

Ahead lay the tempest—the night winds.

For an instant he was afraid to release the wounded kite, afraid the winds would destroy it, but then shadows flicked across the moons, and he knew he had no choice. He gripped the torn tail.

"Take me home," he gasped.

He tossed the kite aloft.

BANG—the winds caught the sails, whirring through the rips. Somehow the sails didn't tear further, and captured enough wind to jerk the kite up—

And Oliver with it. He leapt forward, throwing himself fearlessly into the winds, he and the crimson kite at one with the maelstrom. Last night, he had resisted the night winds, but tonight he allowed them to hurl him toward the peak, reveling in their power and fury. His boots pounded the grass, his strides lengthening as his speed increased.

Three more hunters dove, silhouetted by the moons.

They buzzed past, talons slashing, but all three strikes missed as Oliver raced up, up, up, staggering to the peak as his lungs wept for air and his legs begged for mercy.

They reached the peak. The ascent continued without pause.

Now Oliver was flailing above the ground toward the oakline. He caught a glimpse of circling hunters, but their strikes were hopeless now, hurtling by above and below but not managing another hit. Oliver would have screamed in triumph if he were able.

But as he banged along at the end of the kite's torn tail, he realized that they weren't rising fast enough. The oaks and their hard, mostly bare branches were approaching alarmingly fast. And he realized, from the way the kite flew and the way its tail had not wrapped around his arm, that the kite did not have the strength to carry him much higher.

Oliver's shin struck the first branch with a thundering crack.

Then the winds blew in and seized them and threw them higher, above the oaktops. They flew over Lord Gilbert's treehouse, ablaze with light. Oliver could see hunter silhouettes firing past below. They had abandoned the hunt. In the open winds, he was safe. He managed a grin through the horrible pain in his shoulder, back, legs, arms, and head.

I did it! he thought triumphantly.

FLASH

Uh-oh, he thought less triumphantly.

FLASH

The hunt was not over.

FLASHFLASHFLASH

Each flash shot a bolt of agony through his skull.

FLASH

In the blazing lights of Lord Gilbert's treehouse, Oliver could see the hunters firing in straight lines, directly at the disc beneath the riven oak.

He hadn't escaped at all, not yet anyway. Lord Gilbert was sending the hunters after him.

He clung to the kite's tail with both hands, wishing he could feel it wrapped around his arm again. The kite flew raggedly as the night winds carried them ever higher. He worried that the crimson kite, in its damaged condition, might not find its way into the void between worlds. But soon they entered the mist, and then its cold damp added a chill to the list of Oliver's discomforts.

He looked automatically at the handvane. It insisted on pointing in the wrong direction, directly opposite the flow of wind. *Useless,* thought Oliver. He gave it an awkward shake, but the pointer was adamant in its wrongness. He'd have to get Great-uncle Gilbert to fix it too, once he found him. . . .

If he found him.

He noticed something dismaying.

He seemed to be a little farther away from the kite than he'd been before. His hands, slick with sweat, were slipping down the tail. He tried to pull himself up, hand over hand, but that made him slip even more. Flutters of panic began—he tried to tighten his grip, but there wasn't much to hold on to. He did not look down— there was nothing to see but mist—but he realized he was alarmingly close to falling.

Within moments there was only an inch or two of tail left. Oliver grasped desperately, trying to wrap the tail around his wrist as the kite had done, trying to make some kind of knot.

He slipped through the loose loop he had made. Any second now he would fall, and the kite would fly on—

The loop tightened.

Startled, and relieved beyond measure, Oliver looked hopefully at the kite. "Was that you?" he shouted over the winds.

There was no hint of a reply.

They suddenly pitched downward, roughly, almost as though they were going to land. Oliver was surprised. Last night it had taken them much longer to fly between the two Windblownes.

Abruptly, the mist vanished, and the ground filled his vision, a vast shadow expanding with sickening speed.

He slammed into the ground, rolling, crying out as the rolling took him over his many slashes and bruises. When he stopped, he could feel his shirt clinging wetly to his back.

He sat up, hugging the kite. *Home.* He ached all over, but he didn't care. He wasn't dead. He wasn't held captive in another world. He was home. The two moons gleamed, the familiar crest spread around him, and somewhere below, his family and treehouse waited for him.

"Home," Oliver whispered to the kite. He stood,

wincing, and scanned the night sky. No hunters—not yet, anyway.

He shivered a little. No hunters—and no night winds, either, he noticed. Though he stood in the middle of the crest, he could hardly feel any wind at all. The air was dead calm. The night was perfectly quiet.

"Maybe I'm just getting used to the winds," he whispered, then shook his head irritably. That was ridiculous, and why was he whispering, anyway? He wasn't in any danger, at least for the moment—was he? Something felt wrong.

He peered around in the darkness, which was beginning to lift. Dawn was breaking.

Dawn on the day before the Festival of Kites, he realized. He'd almost forgotten.

The feeling of wrongness grew. The light of dawn was revealing something below, something on the oakline.

Oliver gasped. He turned in a slow circle, taking everything in.

Though he stood on the peak of the mountain, he could not see a single oak. He couldn't see anything of Windblowne at all. Surrounding him, surrounding the entire crest in a great circle where the oakline ought to have been, rose an immense and towering wall.

13

"Is this the hell-world?" whispered Oliver.

His kite trembled faintly.

No, this couldn't be the hell-world. The sun was warm, the morning sky clear and blue, the air cool; dew lay on the grass. A pleasant midsummer day. Birds were here, chirping optimistically. Nothing seemed wrong or out of place besides the lack of wind, and the wall.

Actually, besides the wall, there wasn't much to see. It dominated everything, completely enclosing the crest in stone. Along its west face, the early-morning sun glinted off the smooth granite. The east face threw a shadow that covered most of the crest. A few bare oak branches became visible on the other side, their highest points waving gently over the top. So there was wind outside the wall.

Oliver tried to guess the sheer quantity of granite required to build something like this. The wall had to be extraordinarily thick and strong to withstand the night winds. Its foundations must be deeply rooted in the mountain. Whatever the amount, it was a lot, and there didn't appear to be a single door or any stairs or any other way off the crest. He and the kite were trapped.

Pain flared in his back. If the hunters . . .

Quickly, he scanned the sky.

He saw no hint of the ominous dark forms. But he was certain they would come. Two had said they could track the kite now.

Oliver held up his kite. "I'm going to stop Lord Gilbert," he promised, hoping for a response. Was that a little nod? It was hard to tell. At any rate, he had to get off the crest. He hurried toward the base of the wall, one eye on the sky.

The closer he got, the more the wall towered over him, dispelling the faint hope that he had returned to his own Windblowne and the townspeople had simply decided to build a giant wall in his absence. Something on this scale would take many years to build. Obviously, the kite did not have the strength to guide him home. This meant they were simply blundering from world to world. And there were many, many worlds, Lord Gilbert had said. . . .

Oliver shivered.

He wished he could get some use out of his great-uncle's handvane, but it was still pointing in the wrong direction. The wrong direction was hard west, which was a little ridiculous considering there was no wind at all. He tried to give it a twirl, but it insisted on west. "Fine," Oliver muttered. He removed it and dropped it into his pack.

At least his bleeding had stopped, and the blood seemed to be caking up on the back of his shirt quite nicely, so he didn't have that uncomfortable wetness anymore. *There,* he thought, darkly cheered. *It's not all bad.* Sure, his body ached with every step, but the headache that had plagued him in Lord Gilbert's Windblowne was gone. He could listen to the winds again without fear.

Oliver hurried on. He arrived at the wall and was met with a blast of wind.

He staggered, then found his footing and straightened. Why was there wind here? His eyes roamed over the curve of the wall. Something about its shape must direct whatever wind leaked in, accelerating it so that it ran around the edges in a powerful stream.

He looked up again, bracing himself, feeling dizzy. The wall seemed to lean over him, impossibly tall. The wind swept around, making an empty, hollow moan.

On top of the wall, something moved.

Oliver whipped his head toward the motion. For an instant, out of the corner of his eye, he thought he had seen someone with long hair, leaning over. If it had been there, it was gone.

"I'm imagining things again," he whispered to the kite.

The kite offered no opinion.

He smacked his lips, noticing that his throat was parched. He recalled hearing once that blood loss makes you thirsty. The information hadn't seemed relevant to his life at the time.

He felt something soft snaking around his wrist and yelped.

He slapped at his arm, thinking *Snake!,* then, feeling rather foolish, realized it was only the kite's tail, which meant—

YANK!

His arm was nearly pulled from its socket—again—

and he found himself being swept upward, out of control, banging against the hard granite as he went. In ten painful seconds he found himself tumbling over the upper edge of the wall; then the pressure on his arm was released, and he was falling. Somehow he was able to turn his body and land semi-gracefully on top of the wall, rolling onto his back. He stared up at the blue sky. *Not bad,* he thought. *I'm getting the hang of that.*

He sat up and looked for his kite.

It lay a few feet away, flat on the stone, rippling faintly in the gentle breeze.

He crawled over to it. "Hey," he said uncertainly. He gave it a poke but got no response besides the weary ripple. Whatever energy it had used to get him up the wall was completely exhausted. "Thank you," Oliver whispered. He gathered the kite into his arms and looked around.

The wall curved majestically around the crest, dwindling away to tiny points in both directions. It was about ten feet thick. Everything was quiet, except for a soft hush of wind and a few distant chirps. *At least there are birds here,* Oliver thought. He could guess now why there were no birds on Lord Gilbert's Windblowne. They had all fled from the hunters.

"Why would they build this wall?" he whispered. The kite lay limply in his hands, unresponsive. And why was he still whispering, he asked himself. Something about this Windblowne made him whisper.

Summoning his courage, he stood and crossed to the other side of the wall, half interested in and half frightened by what he might see.

Below him, spilling down to the distant foothills, was a perfectly normal Windblowne. There were all of the familiar treehouses of neighbors and shops and schoolmates. Tiny dots of townspeople were hurrying along Windswept Way. The light wind brought with it the sounds of a living town—the murmur of voices, the pealing of a water clock as it sounded the half hour, the knocking of hammers as they repaired damage from the winds. He could even see the Volitant Dragon. He smiled. Windblowne had never looked so good.

All seemed well in the town, other than the partly leafless oaks. The effects of Lord Gilbert's machine were becoming more evident. Oliver could see through bare patches in many of the trees.

"Here's the plan," Oliver whispered to the kite. He stopped, then spoke in a normal voice. "Here's the plan.

I'll climb down, hurry into town, and find the mayor."
He thought of the mayor complaining about his mother's
sculptures. "No, the mayor is a fool. And the Watch is
useless. I'll find the great-uncle Gilbert from this world
and warn him. Maybe he can help." It was a hasty plan,
but it would have to do.

There was also the matter of breakfast. The wind
brought with it the smell of food cooking all over the
mountain. Oliver felt as though he could eat an entire
side of bacon and a few dozen eggs, all by himself. He
leaned over the edge and looked down at the dizzying
drop. Quickly deciding that he was not willing to jump
off and hope the kite could carry him down safely, he
began to hunt around for other means of descending. He
saw nothing except a few oak branches, swaying gently
just within reach.

Like anyone from Windblowne, a few days earlier he
would never have considered climbing an oak. It was far
too dangerous. But Oliver had done a lot of dangerous
things in the past few days, and something as innocuous
as descending an oak unaided didn't seem that perilous
any longer.

He removed his pack and fastened the kite to the

kite straps, then hurried along the lonely curve of wall until he found a sturdy branch poking over. He hopped on. The branch swayed under his weight as he wriggled his way to the trunk. Oliver was surprised to discover that tree climbing was rather fun, and not really that dangerous—although he wouldn't want to be up there during the night winds. He climbed down through the wide-spreading branches. There was no sign of Windswept Way, but he knew that if he muddled down-slope he would come across it soon enough. With the wall blocking the route to his destination, he had no choice but to use the main road.

He crashed through the forest, wading through mounds of oak leaves.

He had not been crashing for long before he heard familiar, unpleasant voices. Voices that made him want to retreat into the trees. He braced himself. "I've got nothing to be scared of," he whispered to the kite. "I've been through worse than this."

He peeked out from behind the nearest oak. He saw a duplicate Marcus and a duplicate Alain and a few other nasty faces from school. They were shuffling along oddly, heads down, as though they had not noticed the beautiful day. A few were looking up worriedly at the oaks. There was no duplicate Oliver among them—and why would there be? Oliver was never welcome among their counterparts in his own Windblowne. Looking up and down the Way, he saw a few other Windblownians, mostly adults, shuffling, oblivious to midsummer and to the fact that there ought to be a Festival going on.

But of course, there was no Festival here. Not with that wall.

Maybe this is a bad idea, Oliver thought uneasily. But he had to brave the town sooner or later.

Steeling himself, he stepped onto the Way.

Oliver expected the usual laughs and ridicule. Instead, the group stared at him in surprise. "Hey!" Marcus said. "Who are you?"

The plan was not going well.

"Uh," said Oliver, thinking fast. "I'm Oliver One—I mean, I'm Oliver."

There was a collective gasp. "Don't be a jerk," Marcus snapped, balling one hand into a fist. Alain joined him, looking just as angry.

"That's not funny," said Alain. "Whoever you are, you'd better get off our mountain."

Marcus and Alain closed in, fists up. Oliver backed away, congratulating himself on his brilliant strategy.

"Sorry," he pleaded, waving his hands defensively, "I, uh . . ." He turned to run.

There was another collective gasp; then a voice from the back of the group squeaked, "A KITE!"

Oliver turned back in surprise. Marcus and Alain were retreating, and now it was their hands that were waving in defense.

That's better, thought Oliver. He slipped the kite from its straps and held it high. "Yes, it's a kite!" he announced. "Do you like it?" He whooshed the kite dramatically around his head.

The response was a satisfying scattering of his tormentors. One or two of them screamed. "We're telling the Watch!" Marcus yelped, and ran.

Oliver watched as they disappeared down the Way. *That,* he thought, *was the weirdest thing yet.* He held up the kite for inspection. "How did you do that?" he asked. "You need to teach me that trick." The kite seemed to shiver—or was it the wind?

Oliver chuckled at the thought of the others alerting the Watch. Was he supposed to be scared? He had faced killer hunters and mad geniuses. The Watch was no threat to him. By the time those fat old men finished their ample breakfasts and puffed their way up the mountain, he would have had plenty of time to get to Great-uncle Gilbert's treehouse on this world.

As for getting to the treehouse . . . He looked around. The Way had emptied. Oliver was not sure what was going on here, but clearly he stuck out in his flying clothes. There was no help for that, but he had to make his way around a bit more carefully. He'd have to abandon the Way, and stick to the forest, and—

"HALT!" a powerful voice shouted. "Halt in the name of the Windblowne Watch!"

Oliver whirled around.

A group of men were running up the Way—young, strong men. They reached him before he could recover from his shock. Oliver recognized them all. In his own Windblowne, each of them was a promising young flier, the kind of man who hoped to be a champion someday. But here they were dressed in the uniforms of the Watch.

The Watchmen circled him, keeping a wary distance.

"Listen!" Oliver said quickly. "I know what's wrong with the oaks. I—"

One of the men was wearing captain's colors. "Drop the kite!" he ordered.

"But—"

"Drop it!" shouted the captain. He stepped closer, a hand moving to his hip. Oliver saw that he was carrying a club.

Everything was silent but for wind caressing the oaks and, far off, a swallow's sudden cry.

"Yes, sir," said Oliver meekly. "Sorry," he whispered to the kite as he set it carefully on the ground.

"Now step away!" the captain ordered, his muscles bulging authoritatively under his uniform. Unlike the rumpled uniforms of the Watch in Oliver's Windblowne, these men's outfits were crisp and pressed and fit perfectly.

Oliver thought they were being a little silly but felt it would be better not to tell them this. He stepped away from the kite.

The captain looked around at the other Watchmen. "Bear," he said to the largest and strongest-looking. "Get the kite."

"Uh, captain," Bear said, "I'm not touching that thing." Murmurs of agreement came from the other Watchmen.

The captain grimaced. "Right," he said. "We'll ask the mayor what to do. For now, go to the Goldspar Inn and get a blanket. Toss it over the kite and weigh it down with rocks. We'll deal with it later."

"Good idea, captain!" said Bear, obviously relieved. He ran down the Way.

The captain turned back to Oliver. "You!" he thundered. "You must be from the valley! You think this is some kind of joke?"

"No, sir," Oliver squeaked, "I—"

"That's what I thought!" the captain shouted. "Seize him!"

Oliver was seized. Powerful hands grabbed his arms.

"March him down to headquarters," ordered the captain.

And down the mountain they marched. That is, the Watchmen marched. Oliver dangled. He was hoisted between two of the men and carried off, his feet kicking futilely. Soon they had passed around the first bend and left the kite entirely behind.

14

This wasn't good at all.

Oliver recovered his wits. He was a wind-traveling hero, and he wouldn't be manhandled by a bunch of thugs. "Put me down!" he yelled.

The captain shook his head grimly.

"I said," shouted Oliver, taking a deep breath, "put me down! I haven't done anything!"

The captain rolled his eyes and nodded. The Watchmen released Oliver, and he tumbled to the ground.

"Men," growled the captain, "if the prisoner makes one more sound, gag him."

One of the Watchmen shoved him. "Keep moving!" the shover ordered.

Oliver craned his neck, spotting the Volitant Dragon,

built high in its oak, just like at home. But unlike at home, he didn't see colorful banners flapping in the breeze or excited children with new handvanes running around its balconies. Instead, there were boarded-up windows, peeling paint, and doors hanging off their hinges. The wooden dragon was still swinging from its post, but it had been painted over, roughly, in peeling brown, and read, in crude letters: CLOSED.

A Watchman shoved him forward. "I said keep moving!"

Oliver twisted. "It's the Eighth Day of the Second Moon!"

"You're a smart one," the Watchman sneered.

"Where's my gag?" the captain muttered, patting his pockets.

Oliver couldn't help himself. "What happened to the Dragon? Why isn't there any Festival?"

"Found it!" announced the captain. He jammed a wad of rags into Oliver's mouth. The Dragon soon passed from view.

"Mmph!" Oliver said. He reached for the gag. A Watchman grabbed for him and pinned his arms.

He turned his head in all directions. No kites, no

Festival decorations, no posters littering the streets, no announcements of the day's schedule. The town felt sad and empty without them.

The Windblownians seemed sad and empty, too. A few looked curiously at him, then hurried on, their heads down and their faces troubled.

An intense longing for Windblowne, his Windblowne, filled Oliver. He wished he could see his treehouse again—

Which, of course, he could. He realized with a start that they were nearly there.

His mother did not have her sculptures crowding the lane—there were no sculptures at all. The lawn was clear and neat, just like any other lawn in Windblowne. The treehouse looked the same as ever, if a bit tidier. But his mother's workshop was dark and shuttered, and a padlock hung on the door.

Oliver began to feel sick. He spat the gag from his mouth. "Who lives here?"

"You know who lives here," snapped the captain. "We heard what you told those kids." He bent down for the gag, then drew his hand back in disgust. "Re-gag the prisoner," he ordered one of his men, who glared at Oliver.

"But I—" Oliver began. The damp and now dusty gag cut off his protest.

We must . . . I mean, they must not live here anymore, thought Oliver miserably. Then he saw his father.

Oliver had not recognized him at first. He had never seen his father without his writing journal in hand, scribbling notes for one of his books. Usually he carried a sling stuffed with other books he was using for his research. He walked everywhere slowly, stopping every few steps to write, as some idea struck him.

In this world, though, Oliver's father carried nothing. He still walked slowly, but his head was bent, and his step was heavy. He looked terribly sad, and Oliver had the sudden and very unexpected urge to run to him and comfort him.

Oliver tried to dart between the Watchmen. "Mmph!" he said as loudly as he could.

"I hate this kid," panted the Watchman on his left, fighting for a grip.

They came alongside Oliver's father, who raised his head leadenly to peer at the strange sight of six burly Watchmen struggling to contain one lively boy.

Oliver's eyes bulged as they met his father's. "MMPH!" he cried desperately.

For an instant, his father's heavy eyes cleared and there was a flash of recognition. But then his father shook his head, muttered angrily, and trudged on.

"Mmph," groaned Oliver. He stopped fighting. He felt numb with despair. His own father—sort of—had done nothing to help him. His own father had abandoned him to the Watch. *He's not really my father,* he told himself. *My real father would have helped me.*

They came to Watch headquarters. The gag was yanked from Oliver's mouth.

This headquarters looked as much like the one in Oliver's Windblowne as these Watchmen looked like their fat and beery counterparts. It had bars on the windows and steep stairs on which other young, sharply dressed Watchmen were trotting up and down with serious looks on their faces.

They were the same serious expressions that Oliver had seen on every face in this world. There were no kindly looks, no smiles, no laughter.

Two passing Watchmen were talking urgently. "Leaves

falling all over the mountain," one was saying. "No one knows why."

"I know why!" said Oliver.

The men peered at Oliver. "What did this one do?"

"Came up from the valley," answered the captain. "Dressed like a flier. Called himself Oliver. Thinks he's funny."

Oliver began, "I don't th——"

"Up!" ordered the captain.

Oliver put one foot on the lowest step. He wondered if he was going into a jail cell. Would this be his final glimpse of daylight? He looked up, savoring a last moment of sun and wind and sky. . . .

And saw a little black dot that was rapidly getting larger.

"UP!" demanded the captain.

Oliver whirled and grabbed the captain's shoulders. He pointed, shouting, "A hunter! I mean, a . . . a kite!"

The captain chuckled mirthlessly. "Oh, we're not falling for that. We've heard that one befo——"

A shriek shattered the air as the hunter dove straight at Oliver.

15

Oliver leapt as the hunter struck him a glancing blow. He fell flat on his back, his breath knocked from his body and his head hitting the solid ground. This position gave him an excellent view of the entirely one-sided battle between the Watchmen and the hunter.

The men were shouting and running in all directions as the hunter tore through them, talons flashing. Two Watchmen crawled under the steps near Oliver. Oliver thought he heard one of them whimpering for his mother.

"Men! Remember your training!" the captain shouted, but it was obvious that the training had not included keeping a cool head during a kite attack.

Oliver worked on getting some air back into his lungs as he struggled to his knees.

"Mother," whimpered the steps.

Pathetic, thought Oliver.

The hunter was cutting the air in a low, wicked circle. *It's looking for the kite,* thought Oliver.

He hopped backward a few steps, then turned and fled up the mountain, into the oaks. If he went straight up the slope, he would keep crossing the Way. If he could direct himself properly using his map, he would come out of the woods right where he had left his kite.

He plunged desperately, running when he could, scurrying on all fours where the brush was too thick or the slope was too steep.

He burst from the trees, right onto the open Way, directly into the path of an elderly woman. It was Marcus's grandmother.

"Sorry—" Oliver panted, but the old woman screamed, "It's him! The boy from the valley!"

Great, Oliver thought, *I'm famous.* He had obviously made quite an impression on this Windblowne during his brief visit.

"I never liked you either!" he shouted as she took a swipe with her cane. Then he shot into the forest again.

Oliver smashed along, cursing as he was thwacked in the head by low-hanging branches.

He barreled out onto the Way again, huffing. An excited group of people stood talking nearby. "Four kites!" one of them was saying breathlessly. "They attacked the Watch!"

Wild rumors were spreading. Oliver adopted a casual saunter and walked, panting, hair full of twigs, across the Way.

One of the group looked toward Oliver. "Hey—" he started.

Oliver exploded into a run. Then he was in the oaks again, slipping and crawling upward. In a few frantic minutes he came again to the Way, and this time he raced straight across the road. Now he was really a spectacle, covered with dirt, more leaves, and spiderwebs. But this time no one looked at him.

"A whole fleet of them!" someone was shouting. "A whole fleet of kites appeared and demolished Watch headquarters! They're plucking up the Watch and carrying them off!"

Oliver wished that were true.

Closer to the crest now, the mountain was getting

steeper. His running felt more like an excruciating plod. Bright spots flashed in front of his eyes.

He hurtled onto the Way for the fourth time, wild-eyed, chest heaving. The kite was just a little higher. He would have to risk running on the open Way.

As he ran, he heard the shouts of the Watchmen. They had taken the long way around, but they were also much faster.

Ahead, a crowd had gathered at the place where he'd been forced to abandon his kite. With relief, Oliver saw a blanket on the ground. Someone had covered the kite, just as the captain had ordered. The crowd was keeping a wary distance from the blanket.

"HALT!" The Watchmen were right behind him.

Oliver ran through the startled crowd, tossed away the blanket, and seized the kite.

"A kite!" someone screamed. The crowd stumbled backward, bumping and pushing.

Oliver whirled around crazily, shouting, "A kite! A kite! Ha ha!" and waving the kite about like a sword, feeling utterly ridiculous.

The Watchmen shoved their way through the panicked

crowd. But even they would not come close to the madly whirling Oliver.

A piercing scream tore through the air. The hunter had found them.

This was too much for the timid citizens of this Windblowne, and they scattered like leaves. The Watchmen scattered with them.

Oliver ran into the forest. He heard a whir as the hunter sliced through the air.

His chest seemed to think it wasn't getting enough air. *If I had known what was coming,* Oliver thought, *I would have gotten more exercise.*

Somewhere above, the hunter screeched angrily. Oliver looked up, trying to spot the hunter, trying to—

WHACK

He ran smack into the wall. Luckily, he had not been going very fast.

Gasping, he placed his hands against the solid granite. He turned his face up, looking at the wall's vast height— and realized he was out of options.

He searched for a rock, a branch, anything he could use as a weapon.

There was a soft squawk. Trembling, Oliver turned.

The hunter was perched on a nearby limb, regarding him with its glass eyes. Oliver put his hand on the heaviest branch he could find and prepared to defend his kite.

Then something whirred through the air and struck the branch on which the hunter was perched. The hunter gave a startled croak and hopped aside. When another object—Oliver thought it was a stone—followed the first, the hunter had to leap from the branch.

A barrage of stones came whizzing one after another. The hunter shrieked, made two fast circles, and then, with a bright flash, disappeared.

Oliver swallowed hard. "It's gone to get the others," he said, pulling the kite close. A slight breeze rose, and the kite's tail flew up and stroked his arm.

He looked up, trying to find the source of the stones. At first he didn't see anything or anyone. Then there was a sudden movement on a high branch deep within a nearby oak, a movement like the one that he had seen when he first arrived in this Windblowne. He spotted a shadow, crouching on a hidden branch, high above him.

The shadow spoke.

16

"What was that? That wasn't a bird!" the shadow said.

Oliver recognized the voice. *Oh no,* he thought. *Not her. I lost her kite charm.*

The shadow melted down through the oak, climbing swiftly. Soon the light revealed a girl, wiry and small, with black hair tied back and a splash of freckles on her face, and a red knit pouch slung over her shoulder. She swung one-handed onto a branch twenty feet above Oliver's head and crouched there, looking at him curiously and tossing a round stone from one hand to the other.

It was Ilia. Oliver wished he could melt into the ground. Then he realized that, in this Windblowne, she had no idea who he was or that he had been so careless as to lose her charm. In fact, it wasn't even *her* charm.

She also didn't know that Oliver had once, through extreme ineptitude, destroyed her most beautiful kite. She didn't know that, in another world, people still spoke ruefully of the school of flying fish that shattered into a thousand pieces after Oliver accepted the reels.

Some of the white-hot embarrassment faded away. "No," Oliver answered finally. "It wasn't a bird. Well, most of it, anyway."

Ilia continued to stare. Oliver became uncomfortably aware of his appearance. His flying clothes looked as if they had been shredded by wild animals, which they had, with help from half the thornbushes on the mountain. They were blood-soaked and filthy, like the rest of him. His kite was a perfect match, battered and covered in dust. It was said in Windblowne that people end up looking like their kites. For Oliver, this had never been more true.

"Can I see your kite?" Ilia asked.

"Uh," said Oliver.

Ilia seemed to take that as a yes. Slinging the stone into the red knit pouch, she descended, skipping from branch to branch. She landed with a thump beside Oliver and reached out.

Oliver, surprised that she did not seem afraid, held out the kite.

She poked it cautiously. A delighted smile broke out on her face. "What a nice kite!" she said.

"You have no idea," said Oliver, feeling proud.

"I might," said Ilia. "I was sitting on the wall this morning, watching the sun rise. I saw you fly down from the sky. I've been following you ever since."

"Oh," said Oliver.

"You need some help with your oak climbing," said Ilia.

"Well, it was my first try," Oliver said defensively. "How did you follow me?"

"Through the oaks," replied Ilia. She took another stone from her pouch and scanned the sky. "So is that . . . thing . . . coming back?"

"It's called a hunter. And yes. It's going to bring more with it."

"Come on, then," said Ilia. She turned and dashed along the wall. Oliver followed, listening for signs of pursuit from below.

They soon came to an oak with several low-hanging branches. Without breaking stride, Ilia began to climb.

Oliver fastened the kite to his pack and climbed after her, glad that she had gone first. He wanted to practice climbing some more before she saw him at it again.

The air seemed to get thinner as they climbed, or maybe Oliver was reaching the physical limits of exhaustion. He felt queasy. He wondered how long it would take him to hit the ground if he fell, how many branches he might hit on the way down. Ilia showed no signs of tiring, and he wasn't about to ask her to slow down.

Don't look down, Oliver thought. This made him look down. As he suspected, the ground was now quite far below, with plenty of branches in the way. When he turned back, Ilia had disappeared. There was nothing above him but an impenetrable tangle of branches and clusters of dead or dying leaves.

"Ilia?" Oliver ventured.

Leaves rustled. He heard a shout, far off.

"Ilia?" Oliver whispered nervously. Had she fallen?

"Hurry up!" Ilia's voice snapped from above. "I can see them coming!"

Then Oliver saw it—the slightest break in the tangle, just to his right. He climbed over and up, fast as he could, and clambered through a cleverly concealed trapdoor and into a small, snug treehouse.

Ilia was peering into a miniature brass telescope that pointed through a tiny window.

"Who's coming?" Oliver wheezed, glad to feel a solid floor beneath him. "The hunters?"

"No," said Ilia. "Just some of the Watch."

"What will we do? We're trapped!"

"Don't worry," Ilia replied. "I've got this treehouse entirely camouflaged."

Oliver looked all around, marveling. The treehouse was large enough for both of them to move about comfortably. There were open crates scattered around that were full of interesting things like ropes and pulleys and gears and more telescopes, and even a bow and some arrows. There were more throwing stones for the red knit pouch, and a threadbare rug on the floor, some dry food, a few canteens, and candles. Windows looked in all directions, and there was another window in the roof, covered by a sliding door.

"Who built this?" said Oliver in wonder. "It's amazing."

"I did," said Ilia, beaming. "I've been working on it a little bit at a time, for years."

"And no one knows about it?"

"Nope," said Ilia. "You're the first. Do you really like it?"

"Yes," said Oliver. Suddenly he had the feeling he might be blushing. He grabbed one of the telescopes and fumbled with it. "I bet you can see whatever goes on in Windblowne from up here."

"Well, I can see a lot of things. Especially now, because the oaks have been losing their leaves. Everyone is trying to pretend that nothing's wrong, but I'm really worried."

"I am, too," said Oliver.

"They think the wall is going to protect them from everything," Ilia muttered.

Oliver settled on a pillow, stretching out his aching legs. "Yes, the wall," he said. "What is that for?"

"You don't know?" said Ilia skeptically. "Where are you from, anyway?"

"I'm, uh, from the valley."

"Hmmm," said Ilia. "You're from the valley, and you made a kite that could fly in the night winds, and you flew over the wall with it this morning?"

"Yes?" lied Oliver.

Ilia raised one eyebrow. "Pretty impressive for someone from the valley."

"I could have gotten this kite from Windblowne," Oliver suggested. "Maybe I didn't make it myself."

She stared at him. "Don't you know that no one here makes kites anymore? I was six years old when they started building the Crest Wall, and that was the last time I saw a kite in the sky. I can still remember it."

"Why did they build it? Why stop people from flying kites?"

Ilia lowered her eyes. "Because of the Lost."

"Who are the Lost?" Oliver asked.

She sat heavily on a pillow, tossing her pouch next to the pile of stones.

"Something happened," she began. "Years ago, just before the Festival of Kites. A group of children were flying their kites on the crest. A big gust of wind blew up, and somehow one of the children was carried away. Everyone shouted for him to let go of his kite, but he refused. He disappeared into the sky."

"I see," said Oliver.

"They searched for him for days, all through the valley and the plains, trying to find where he might have come down. There was no sign of him anywhere. His parents were frantic." As Ilia told the story, her face became weary, with the same sad expression that Oliver had seen on the faces of so many townspeople below.

Oliver thought about his family's treehouse, and the shuttered workshop, and his father's downcast face. He had a very good idea of the name of the boy who had been blown away by the winds. "Did . . . that boy . . . make the kite himself?"

Ilia looked at him strangely, then shook her head. "No. His great-uncle, a famous master kitesmith, made it for him. Everyone went to him after the boy disappeared, but his great-uncle had no idea what had happened. He searched as hard as anyone for his grandnephew."

Oliver swallowed. "And they built the wall because of that?"

"No," said Ilia. "They built the wall because of what happened next."

Muffled shouts came from below. Ilia and Oliver ran to the windows.

"Have they found us?" Oliver said anxiously.

"No," whispered Ilia, telescope to eye. "They're just searching the forest. Keep your voice down."

They sat back on the pillows. "So what happened next?" prompted Oliver.

"Several nights later," Ilia continued solemnly, "four more children disappeared. Their parents went to wake them in the morning, and their beds were empty."

Oliver thought of his empty bed, back in a Windblowne that seemed very far away.

Ilia crawled to one of the crates and rummaged. She handed Oliver a piece of paper, old and crumpled.

He opened it and read:

> Come to the crest at midnight.
> Don't tell anyone. I'll explain later.
> —O

The note was in his handwriting.

"They found one of these notes in the room of one of the Lost—after he disappeared," said Ilia. "His flying clothes were gone, just like the other three. None of them were ever seen again."

"And they built the wall because of that?" asked Oliver.

"Partly," Ilia said, "but also because of what happened next."

Oliver waited.

"Windblowne went crazy," Ilia said. "They blamed the great-uncle. The Watch—they were all old men back then—went to his treehouse to arrest him. When they got there, he was packing. He said he was going to search for the children. The Watch tried to stop him, and that's where the story gets really weird. The Watch claimed they were attacked by kites. Some said it was five kites, some said ten—and some said it was really only one. Whatever happened, when they returned, they were covered in bites and bruises and there were a few broken arms."

Oliver thought about the kite-eater, far away in his Windblowne. By now, it had probably chewed most of the way through those books.

Ilia went on. "And the great-uncle was gone. No one ever found him, or the kites, or the children. But after that, everything in Windblowne changed. Everyone became afraid. They built the wall to keep anyone from going to the crest, and they destroyed every kite they could find. They said kites, the same ones that had attacked the Watch, had stolen the Lost away, and that no kites would be allowed in Windblowne again."

"But the kites didn't steal them," Oliver pointed out. "The notes told them to come to the crest!"

"Yes," she sighed. "But they destroyed the note they found, too. They wanted to blame someone, so they blamed the great-uncle and his kites and ignored everything that told another story."

Oliver shook his head. No wonder the other children had gotten so angry with him when he claimed to be Oliver.

"I miss him," Ilia said. "He was my best friend. Everyone said he must be dead, but his great-uncle said he wasn't and that he would be able to find him. But nobody would listen." She paused, studying Oliver, studying his kite. "I know this is a stupid question," she said, hesitating, "but . . . you look a lot like . . . I mean, it's been five years but . . ." Her voice trembled. "Are you Oliver?"

"Yes," said Oliver. "And no. Not your Oliver."

He told Ilia everything, from the moment he had first met Great-uncle Gilbert to his escape from Lord Gilbert's Windblowne. Ilia, at first stunned into silence, became increasingly excited as the tale went on.

At last she burst out, annoyingly, just as Oliver was coming to the part where he bravely fought off a flock of Lord Gilbert's hunters. "This means," she exclaimed, her eyes bright, "that when Oliver . . . I mean, my Oliver . . . disappeared, he traveled to another world!" She jumped to her feet, beaming. "Maybe he's the Oliver who's living with Lord Gilbert!"

"No," said Oliver. "He's lived in that Windblowne his whole life. His parents disappeared along with everyone else."

"Oh," said Ilia, disappointed. "Well, you travel to lots of worlds! You'll find him!"

Oliver shook his head, wishing he could get back to the part where he knocked two hunters aside with a single blow. "No, I'm sorry. I think there's a lot of these worlds—thousands . . . millions. And I can't choose where I go. Not with a broken kite."

"That means . . . ," said Ilia, then paused. "That means when you leave, you'll never come back again?"

Oliver was certain he detected a quaver in her voice.

"No," said Oliver, as manfully and courageously as he could manage. "I don't think so."

"But the kite can still do things," Ilia pointed out. "I saw it carry you up the wall. And you said it grabbed you around the arm before you took off from Lord Gilbert's world."

"Y-yes," said Oliver, thinking, stroking the kite. "It's still alive. But I think it takes a lot of energy and wind before it can do those things, and it's exhausted afterward." He looked at Ilia. It all sounded so weird, he had stopped expecting anyone to believe him. But she sat gazing at him solemnly. There was no doubt that she trusted him. He remembered another Ilia trusting him once before too, and winced before continuing. "And it can't guide me to the right Windblowne. We just have to go wherever the wind takes us. I thought I could use my great-uncle's handvane for guidance, but it's broken, too."

He took Great-uncle Gilbert's handvane from his pack.

Ilia gasped. "A handvane! I haven't seen one in years. And it's so beautiful!"

"Here," said Oliver.

Ilia traced her finger over the intricate carvings. "You have so many amazing things."

Oliver had not thought about it. "I guess I do," he said, trying to boast a little bit but not too much.

Ilia spun the vane, which settled firmly on west. "How would this help guide you between worlds?"

"I don't know," Oliver admitted. "I just thought it

might. I mean, handvanes can tell you a lot of things, like when the winds are about to change, and where the next winds might come from. And Great-uncle Gilbert made this one, so . . ." He shrugged. "Anyway, it's no good."

"I think it's pretty good," said Ilia, smiling and returning the handvane. Oliver placed it back in his pack, more carefully this time.

"So what are you going to do next?" asked Ilia.

"Well," said Oliver slowly, "I'm trying to find my great-uncle, but I don't know how to find him or if I ever will. I'll just have to go from world to world, trying to find where Lord Gilbert left him, and then maybe I can stop Lord Gilbert in time to save the oaks and the other Windblownes and Olivers and . . ." To his shame, his voice was shaking. But when he put it all out like that, the situation sounded hopeless. Anyone who paid attention could tell the oaks were dying, and there wasn't much time left.

He tried to recover his manly tone, but he did not feel manly anymore. He felt like just another Oliver who had been blown away from home.

He looked at the crumpled note, which was both

familiar and foreign at the same time. "Why would those kids do what your Oliver told them?" he asked, thinking that if he wrote such a note, everyone would pass it around, laughing about how his family got weirder every day. They certainly wouldn't light out for the crest at midnight under perilous circumstances.

"Oh, of course they would!" said Ilia, surprised. "Why wouldn't they? I mean, you and your family were just about the most respected people in Windblowne! Probably still are, in your world."

"Er . . . yes," said Oliver. "Of course. Just checking."

Great, he thought. One Oliver is a master kitesmith, the next a legendary leader of men. Well, children. Still, it looked like he was just about the weakest Oliver out there.

He looked at the note again, the childish scrawl somehow infused with greatness. Then something occurred to him.

"The notes," he said, holding up the crumpled paper. "You said they destroyed the one they found. They didn't find this one?"

"No," she said. "They didn't."

"Why not? Whose was it?"

Ilia's face went tight. "It was mine."

"Yours? But—"

"I never saw it," she said bitterly. "I snuck out that night to climb trees. When I came in that morning, the note was on my pillow. But it was too late. Midnight had passed. I was meant to be one of the Lost"— her voice caught—"but now I'll never know what happened."

A few minutes of silence passed. Ilia stared at the floor. Oliver toyed with one of the telescopes, feeling embarrassed. The Oliver of this world had been Ilia's best friend. A best friend would probably know what to say in a situation like this. But he had no idea, any more than he knew how to fix the crimson kite.

The silence was broken by a distant, echoing shout.

"The Watch again," said Ilia, standing. "Don't worry, they've never found my treehouse."

"But they'll keep looking for me," said Oliver. "And if they don't find me, then the hunters will. It will be a lot harder to hide from them."

It was true. The hunters would continue their relentless search, and eventually they would find him. He couldn't protect the crimson kite forever, or his family, or his Windblowne. Wherever he flew, he would bring danger to everyone he met, just like he was bringing danger to Ilia now.

"Maybe we *could* hide from the hunters," said Ilia, growing excited. "I could camouflage the roof, too. You could live in my treehouse! I could bring you anything you needed. They'd never find you!"

Oliver shook his head. "Thank you," he said with regret. "But no. I can't hide. I have to find Great-uncle Gilbert."

Ilia opened her mouth again, then closed it and turned away.

She stepped over to one of the crates and rummaged. At last she found a piece of fabric, which she handed to Oliver. "If you ever do find my Oliver, will you give him this? It's a piece of the tail from a kite his great-uncle flew to win the Festival Grand Prize, decades ago. It was a gift to him, and it was his proudest possession. I . . . I want him to have a memory of home. I want him to know that I miss him."

Oliver accepted the aged piece of silk reverently. "I will," he promised.

"One more thing," said Ilia. She rummaged again. This time she produced a kite charm. "For luck," she said.

Oliver looked at the charm. *Ilia*. "Thank you," he said with the deepest gratitude, and put it carefully into a buttoned inside pocket.

He stayed at the treehouse until dark, he and Ilia taking turns watching the skies through telescopes. While he took a much-needed nap, Ilia ran into town for food to replenish his supplies.

"The whole town is in chaos," she giggled when she returned. "They're saying the kites are back, and everyone's hiding indoors."

Oliver laughed.

When night drew near, Ilia led him up through the oak to a place where he could climb onto the Crest Wall. "This is where I come to watch the sun rise," she told him. "It's where I first saw you."

Oliver stood on the wall, shivering. He could feel the night winds coming. Because Ilia was watching, he took Great-uncle Gilbert's handvane from his pack and snapped it on his wrist. Wearing it did make him feel better, even if it was pointing perpendicular to the winds. His kite seemed to sense the night winds too, its silks rustling as the winds grew stronger and whirls of oak leaves filled the purple twilight.

"You'd better go," he said to Ilia.

She nodded and leapt into her oak, swinging down toward the safety of her treehouse as she went. "Goodbye!" she shouted over the rising wind. "Goodbye! Goodbye!"

Soon Oliver could no longer hear her voice, and then she was lost from sight.

"Goodbye," said Oliver.

He listened to the wind's roar gathering around the edges of the Crest Wall, pouring up toward him with an animal howl. He shivered again. On his wrist, the hand-vane still pointed resolutely west, no matter how the winds shifted.

"West," Oliver said to the kite. "Why not?" It seemed better to have some kind of plan, even if it relied on a broken handvane.

The kite shook and tugged, ready to fly.

Oliver faced west, kneeling, gripping an outcrop on the wall.

When the sun finally fell, and the full force of the night winds struck, Oliver cast the kite up and flew into the night.

FLASH

FLASH

FLASH

Just in time. The lone hunter had gathered two others, and they'd returned in force.

Together, the crimson kite and Oliver flew through inky darkness. As raggedly as it was flying, the kite still summoned the energy to wrap its tail around Oliver's arm.

Soon they were descending into gentler winds.

He waited for it to get lighter, as it had for his other landings, but everything remained dark. When he glimpsed the grassy crest at last, it was alarmingly close. He lifted his knees and rolled, coming to a perfect sitting position on the grass.

The perfect sitting position did not last long. Night winds blasted, knocking him onto his hands, taking his breath away. He pressed flat against the grass, unable to stand, his arm pulled hard by the wildly bouncing kite.

And it was terribly dark, much darker than it had any right to be at midsummer.

He looked up, searching for a hint of sunrise . . . and gasped.

Above him, the stars winked in their familiar

constellations in their midsummer array. Aspin, the small Second Moon, shone faintly down.

But Aspin was alone.

Nahfa, the larger First Moon and Aspin's companion, was missing from the sky.

17

The night winds threw Oliver about as he tried to crawl in the direction of the oakline. He spent most of the time rolling helplessly. Fortunately, he could still feel his kite, tail tight around his numbing arm as he tumbled.

After a great deal of rolling and smashing, something occurred to Oliver—it didn't hurt at all. So many other things had hurt, like getting knocked into trees and slashed by talons, that Oliver was becoming an expert on ways to experience pain. He would have guessed that getting rolled down the crest by the night winds would have ranked toward the top. But it didn't hurt in the slightest.

The answer came when the winds picked him up and tossed him through two complete flips onto his back. By all rights, he should have broken something—his neck, his back, maybe a leg. But he noticed when he finished the second flip that he didn't hit so much as bounce. He felt around with his hand and discovered that the grass, thin and tough on his own crest, was here thick, lush, and springy, so much so that you could really enjoy the experience once you got over the terror.

This reminded him of the previous night, fleeing the hunters, throwing himself fearlessly into the night winds on his way to the peak. He might be able to do it again. The next time the winds flipped him, he landed on his feet and began running immediately, boots pounding grass, bouncing down the crest.

Oliver was beginning to laugh when he slipped and fell and the winds grabbed him and—

WHAM

Something cracked him in the small of his back. He screamed. The wind took his scream and carried it off. Little bright stars of pain sparked in his eyes.

He grabbed fistfuls of grass and clung stubbornly, waiting for dawn.

He did not have long to wait. The sky lightened, and with it the winds slacked and he was able to relax his death grip. He looked to see what had cracked him.

At first the thing was only a pale spot, buried deep under the thick, waving green. With a little more light, the pale spot became an old stone, an ancient piece of weathered granite. With a bit more light, he realized the stone was fixed into the ground.

The granite jumping marker, worn small and smooth by wind and time, and much too near the crest. By putting his face very close, Oliver could just make out what was left of the inscription:

WIL M ST V

2 o

55

WIL M ST V, Oliver knew, was a name. It was missing some letters, but in any case, it was a flier whom Oliver had never heard of.

2 0 was the record itself, which was definitely missing some numbers.

55 was the year. The year since the founding of Windblowne. This bit was less weathered, and none of the numbers were missing. In Oliver's world, that number

was 405—the date fifty years ago when the record had last been broken.

Here, it was 55.

Which was precisely four centuries ago.

Oliver shivered. In this world, no one had broken the jumping record in all that time. "They must be terrible fliers," he said to the kite, trying to lighten the mood. "I'll be right at home."

Oliver rose to his feet, still in semi-darkness, to see what this new world was like.

The stiff morning carried rich and familiar scents of forest and soil. He could not see the oaks yet, but he could smell them, strong and woody and alive. Just as the grass here was thicker, the smells were also more potent, more vital.

The sunlight grew, and Oliver saw the oaks. They were half again as tall as any oaks he had ever seen. Their leafy tops were lost in low clouds and whirlpools of mist.

Oliver fell to his knees in the grass, closed his eyes, and breathed.

Then he noticed other smells, scents of death and decay and things dark and distant. These smells brought to mind images of the riven oak and its odious, sick scent.

Sounds came on the winds too, but these sounds were very different from the keening cries on Lord Gilbert's world and the hollow moan on the Crest Wall world. Was it music? Singing? Whatever it was, it was sad and sorrowful and it pulled tears from him before he realized it was happening. He wiped his eyes on his sleeve.

Pull yourself together, Oliver!

He got up off his knees.

"I've got to find the Great-uncle Gilbert who lives here," Oliver said to the kite, determined. "I've got to warn him. I'll make sure not to get arrested this time."

The kite gave a *tug* so weak that Oliver thought he imagined it. Then it *tugged* again, and he looked down at his sore and burning arm, where the tail was still wrapped.

He took a couple of curious steps in the direction of the tug.

tug tug

The kite wanted to go somewhere.

Oliver took a few more steps in that direction, as the wind made long, rippling rows in the waving grass. But for the second time in two days, and in his memory, he felt lost. The size of the oaks seemed to have confused his map.

"Wait," Oliver ordered. He turned in all directions, looking, listening.

In the light of morning, with the mist now dissipated, Oliver could see only the towering oaks and lush green grass and dark blue sky, and he could hear only twittering birdsong and windy sighs. There were no signs of any town whatsoever. Oliver had the feeling of being alone in a mysterious, primitive world. He felt a tingling on his skin, and the rich, potent air and the damp golden light seemed to be going to his head. His mind began to swim with wild thoughts that he could run as fast as the wind and stand as tall and as strong as an oak. That he could face down Lord Gilbert and his hunters and anything else that came his way. The air was filled with power, and so was he. He wanted to run and shout and—

tug

Oliver shook his head. He had to keep his wits about him. The truth was, he was wet, cold, lost, and entirely vulnerable should any hunters appear. Any minute now there could be half a dozen flashes and everything would be over for him and the kite and all of the Windblownes. He had to get off the crest, into the shelter of the forest.

"Fine, I'll follow you," he said. "But we have to be more careful this time."

The kite only continued its gentle, wistful tugging.

Oliver allowed the tugging to lead him. He bounced toward the oakline, buzzing from the heady air.

When they reached the oaks, he crouched and peered around, chilled and shivering. Everything was wetter here too, and the rips in what was left of his flying outfit were letting in the water. He rubbed his arms for warmth and tried to get his bearings.

tug

"Wait," whispered Oliver. He checked Great-uncle Gilbert's handvane, still fastened to his wrist. It had survived the rolling without a scratch, though it still pointed off in its own direction, oblivious to the wind. His instruction to fly west did not seem to have produced anything useful. The last two flights had been short—perhaps the kite did not have the strength for a longer trip. His great-uncle could not be in this Windblowne. Lush, green, vibrant, this world was anything but a hell-world.

The morning birds obviously felt the same way. They had started in with earsplitting songs. Oliver was glad that they were happy, but they made it a little hard to think.

He was just wishing they would shut up—

when they did. They shut up instantly, but not before forming a huge black cloud, blotting out the sky, twisting like a tornado. Then the cloud evaporated, leaving an empty sky.

The world was dead quiet.

In the silence, Oliver heard a faraway sound. It was soft, but it had the feel of a sound that would be very loud if you were close by, like a slow, immense, and distant crash.

Something fell, he thought.

Oliver studied the leaves spreading out over his head. He knew this oak. He looked over at the next one—and in that moment, all the surrounding oaks clicked into place on his map. The oaks were far bigger than the oaks in other worlds, but they were still his oaks, the oaks of Windblowne. Oliver knew precisely where he was. He was at the entrance to the secret path.

Or at least, he was at the spot where the entrance

ought to be. The path was not there. There was just more brush, and no sign that anyone had ever cleared away any of it to make his own private way to the crest.

tug

But that was where the kite wanted to go.

Oliver fastened the kite to his pack, leaving its tail on his arm for comfort. Then he drew a long breath—nearly tipping over from the dizziness—and started off into the forest.

That crash had probably been nothing. Nevertheless, he slipped quietly from oak to oak, through the dense, unspoiled forest.

After a while, he noticed he was bouncing again. He had started running and jumping, without being aware of it.

Slow down! he ordered himself.

The burst of energy this world had given him was surging back. He kept wanting to shout. He almost wished he had the Watch captain's gag with him.

Silent, he thought. *Quiet as a shadow.* At least until he knew more about this world. Though his emotions were bobbling all over the place, he tried to concentrate on that single task.

He crept slowly and carefully through more wild forest. Soon he found his great-uncle's oak—

and nothing else at all. He was not surprised to discover that there was no treehouse, of metal or wood. Nothing to indicate a great-uncle of any variety had ever lived here. Just more thick forest all around, and the mournful wind.

He walked closer to the oak. He peered up along the trunk, scanning . . . and then he saw something deep within the gnarled bark of the tree. He pushed his fingers in and felt something cold and rusty. It felt like the head of a bolt, the sort of thing that, once upon a time, might have been used to secure a set of steps.

Great-uncle Gilbert's treehouse—no, this would not have been his treehouse, it would have been someone else's, someone who died long before Great-uncle Gilbert was born. Which he had never been. Not in this Windblowne, anyway. Judging by the jumping marker and the ancient bolt, the Windblowne that had once inhabited this mountain had disappeared centuries ago.

He continued around the oak and saw, for the first time since his arrival, something not filled with vigor and life.

The riven oak.

In this world, it was withered, half the height of its neighbors and bent precariously to one side. Most of its leaves had fallen.

The riven oak in Lord Gilbert's world must be very close to death. Oliver had promised to save the oak. He wasn't doing a very good job.

On his back, the kite had begun to quiver, then thrash about in its straps.

Oliver pulled the kite free, and it flew up on the breeze, beating the air. Oliver had to snatch its tail to keep it from being carried away.

Oliver whooped with joy. He whooped again, his cry echoing through the silent mountain.

His mind raced. Something had brought the crimson kite back to life, but what? The crimson kite's spars were made from the riven oak. Great-uncle Gilbert and Two had used spars from this oak to craft parts of the kite. Close to this oak in this strong, vibrant world, the crimson kite could fly, and who knew what else it—

The kite beat and thrashed, pulling at Oliver.

He whooped a third time, and a fourth, thrilled by the sound of his voice, thrilled at how powerful he sounded as his voice filled the forest, echoing between oaks, primitive and wild.

There was a distant crash. It was a little like the crash he had heard before, except closer.

Oliver went silent.

There was another crash, still distant—but closer still.

He looked around uneasily. He began to wonder why none of the birds had returned.

Another crash. This one even closer.

The crimson kite flew to his side.

Another crash, and something heavy, falling.

Oliver looked around wildly. He bent over and picked up a thick branch that had fallen from the riven oak.

A crash, a crack, and then—

BOOM

Oliver jumped. The smashing sound was steady now, and

SMASH

getting

CRASH

closer. Something immense was coming through the forest, and it was coming fast.

18

Oliver hurtled through the oaks. **Whatever was thundering after him was fast, much faster than he was, and it**

BOOM

was gaining rapidly. Whatever it was, the thing

BOOM

behind him had to be the size of a treehouse—the crashing and cracking sounds

BOOM

were deafening. What could he do? Should he play dead? He remembered hearing that that worked with lowland bears. But the thing behind him was no bear. Bears probably played dead

BOOM

to escape from *it*. In between the sheer terror and

ridiculous mental images of piles of bears playing dead, a desperate thought occurred to him. If it wasn't a bear, then maybe it couldn't climb trees, either. Oliver dodged between oaks, looking at their branches. All of the lowest branches were far above his head. He couldn't possibly

BOOM

climb any of them. But he knew of one oak—Ilia's oak—that had low-hanging branches, if he could just get there before being flattened or devoured or skinned alive

BOOM

or however this thing normally disposed of its prey.

He ran for Ilia's oak as the bellow of the giant creature rolled over him, bringing with it a horribly warm stench. At last he spied the tree, with its unusually low-hanging branches—except that in this world, low-hanging still meant far above Oliver's head.

He snatched the crimson kite from his pack. "I need you. Please," Oliver begged.

He jumped as high as he could, discovering that the fear of being eaten alive can add several inches to your vertical leap. The several inches were of little use, however, and he was on his way back down when the tail snapped taut on his wrist. He shot ten feet straight up and grabbed the lowest branch just as the kite failed and fell. Oliver scrambled furiously upward, trying to be Ilia-like, pulling the kite with him.

WHAM

The oak shuddered and groaned. Oliver clung fiercely, too terrified to look down. A hideous roar shook the tree, and a wave of foul breath enveloped him, making him gag. The oak shook again, and there was another roar.

WHAM

The oak leaned, creaking. Could the crimson kite fly him anywhere else? No, it was exhausted now, draped limply over a branch. He pulled the kite the rest of the way up.

Silence. Oliver took the opportunity to put a few more branches between himself and the ground. He could hear an impossibly heavy tread rumbling around. Loud snorts and a rotting smell came wafting up through the branches. Oliver tried to peer down but could not see a thing through the leafy cover.

What had happened to the branch he'd picked up? He remembered shoving it into his pack right before he started running. And it was still there, poking uncomfortably. He pulled it out, wondering if he should throw it at the creature. He gave it a few practice waves.

The kite shivered on its branch.

Oliver held the branch closer, and the kite shivered a little more.

Even this one piece of the riven oak had a small effect on the kite. It—

WHAM

it didn't really matter, because sooner or later that enormous thing was going to knock him out of the oak and eat him.

rumble rumble

The heavy tread sounded like it was backing up. Oliver braced himself for a tremendous charge, one that would knock him flying from the oak.

A thundering gallop began. He gripped the kite and braced his legs and closed his eyes and—

and then he could not hear the galloping. He couldn't hear anything but an enormous, howling wind, striking from all sides. It was almost as bad as the creature's attacks. Oliver pressed himself against the oak. The winds screamed around him in primal agony, a sound worse than anything Oliver had ever heard, and he screamed, too.

Through his closed eyelids he saw a flash of light, brighter than a thousand hunters appearing at once, explode over the mountain. It faded, and Oliver opened his eyes.

The winds fell, and the galloping sound returned. But this time the gallop was going in the other direction. The creature was running away. Through a small break in the leaves Oliver caught a glimpse of a broad, scaly back disappearing into the brush, leaving behind a path of flattened foliage.

Something had frightened off the monster, and whatever it was, Oliver could feel it, too. Something about this world's living energy, the energy that had made him shout in joy, that had made the birds sing, that had made the oaks grow to wild heights, had vanished.

All around him, the forest was changing color.

For a moment Oliver thought the forest was on fire. All of the leaves were turning yellow and red, as though fire were spreading everywhere at once. As Oliver watched, the yellow and red burned into brown, and then, in a terrible convulsion, the leaves of every oak on the mountain fell in a thick cloud, an ocean of dead leaves. Winter had come in an instant.

If you do whisper, O winds, then whisper to me, of oaks which dwell across the worlds.

Great-uncle Gilbert's strange words, scrawled in that ancient manuscript, came to Oliver. He did not need a whisper to guess that Lord Gilbert, tired of the chase, must have activated the rest of the hunters and was sending them all after Oliver and the kite. The power drain on the oaks was enormous, and now even this world, the strongest and most vital of all the worlds Oliver had visited, was dying.

He took his trembling kite and fastened it to his pack. Into the pack went the riven oak branch, too. And then he dropped swiftly, skipping from branch to branch as he'd seen Ilia do, until he landed on the ground with a thump.

FLASH

FLASH

FLASHFLASHFLASHFLASH

Hunters, Oliver thought, at the same moment he was

diving into the carpet of dead leaves on the forest floor. He wriggled as deep as he could. Six flashes—they were hunting him in sixes now. Six times as dangerous, then.

He waited for hours, breathing in the rich, damp scent of the leaves and listening to the shrieks of the hunters as they searched the mountain. At last there came another FLASH, and then several more, and then no more flashes and no more shrieks. He'd fooled them, but probably not for long.

Oliver crawled from the leaves and ran for the riven oak. He had a plan but didn't have much time before nightfall.

When they reached the oak, Oliver collected as many twigs as he could, pulling them from the ends of hanging branches and stuffing them into his pack. He thought apologies toward the riven oak as the green pieces ripped away.

Dusk was falling as Oliver hurried back to the crest. The twilight winds carried along with them a mountain's worth of dead leaves. As he ran, Oliver felt part of the great whirring, rattling cloud. He almost floated onto the crest, half carried by the winds, holding the kite close.

Oliver looked at Great-uncle Gilbert's handvane. It pointed confidently west.

"West, it is," said Oliver.

He held the kite high. "We have to keep flying west," he said. "Do you understand?"

The kite fluttered, weakly.

Oliver hoped that the bits of the riven oak he'd collected would give the kite the energy to find the way.

The night winds struck, and the kite and Oliver were snatched from the crest.

As they flew through the mist, Oliver imagined he could feel strength flowing from the oak branches in his pack, through his body, and up to the kite, and tried to add to it whatever energy he could.

Carried along by the smooth winds, Oliver dozed off. He woke abruptly when he realized they were descending.

He could hear the kite's sails whirring. The descent was alarmingly fast, and the kite seemed to be struggling to hold them both aloft. When they plunged out of the mist, there were hardly any winds to hold them.

The rough landing sent Oliver tumbling. He rolled professionally, noting that the ground in this world seemed, painfully, to be nothing but hard-packed sand and rock.

He stood up wearily in the semi-darkness. The winds were indeed light, more like night breezes. He could stand on the peak without any effort. He checked the sky and was relieved to see both moons. On the horizon, dawn was beginning to break.

Oliver gasped. The horizon! He had seen the black wires, he'd seen the riven oak, he'd seen the Crest Wall, he'd seen a monster, and he'd seen an entire mountain lose its leaves all at once. But never had he seen anything as awful as he did at that moment.

You did not see actual sunrises in Windblowne. The tall oaks blocked that view in all directions, even on the peak. And so Oliver saw something new—a bump of light becoming a brilliant disc from which he had to look away. An impossibly vast landscape spread out around him, all the way from one side of the world to the other, and all of it was rock and sand, a lifeless desert painted in shades of brown and white. The mountain was rocky and desolate too, and seeing it stretch down on all sides was dizzying. He thought of stories he had heard about sailors in a stormy sea, their ship perched on top of a wave down which they were about to plunge, to be smashed into the ocean. Oliver was struck with that same sense of vertigo, as though he might fall down this mountain and keep falling all the way to the end of the world.

He blinked. The light wind was carrying sand everywhere. Far away, hundreds of miles away over the flat and endless plains, he could see swirling columns of sand moving regally across the distances, carried by the wind. In between them were rock formations as large as cities, with flat tops that looked as though they could hold a dozen crests. In all this overwhelming emptiness, Oliver saw no signs of life.

But as the blazing sun rose, Oliver realized that there was life on the mountain. Starting where the oakline should be were small, twisted things. Fighting vertigo, Oliver stumbled down the crest for a closer look.

The things were oaks. Or at least, something like oaks. They were stunted trees, not much taller than Oliver. Their bark was tough and smooth. They were growing in gaps between the rocks, stretching their wiry limbs in odd, crooked directions. If these were what passed for oaks in this world, then Oliver could not imagine a greater contrast between other worlds and this one.

No use looking for a jumping marker here. This dead

and barren Windblowne had never seen a Festival and never would.

"No one lives here—no one's ever lived here," Oliver said to the kite, which had settled wearily against his leg. "We're all alone." It was a vast and dark sensation.

"Not entirely true," said a voice from behind him.

Oliver whirled. He hadn't expected to see anyone in this wasteland. He especially hadn't expected to see a familiar figure dressed in a robe and carrying a carved walking stick. He hadn't expected to see Great-uncle Gilbert standing with a tired smile on his face, among the withered oaks.

19

The hell-world! Oliver thought. *I found it!* **He** cautioned himself to play it cool, in the manner of the world-class adventurer he had become. "Hullo," he said with an air of breezy confidence. "I'm here to resc——"

"Who or what," interrupted Great-uncle Gilbert, peering closely at Oliver, "are you?"

The poor old man, thought Oliver. The hell-world had driven him mad. Well, madder. "I'm your grand-nephew, Oliver," he explained patiently. "And I'm here to resc——"

"Oliver, eh?" interrupted Great-uncle Gilbert again, peering some more. "I suppose you are, under all that. You look like you've been shot through the woods from a cannon, my boy."

Oliver looked down at himself. True, he was not at his best. His flying outfit was in ruins, and there wasn't much of him that wasn't coated in dirt, leaves, twigs, and goopy substances of mysterious origin. He tried to remember if he had been this disheveled when he had met Ilia. "Well, I can't exactly help it," he said. "I've flown across four worlds to resc—"

"Didn't listen to me, did you?" interrupted Great-uncle Gilbert, shaking his head. "Now you're trapped, too." He sighed in a way that suggested he was resigned to Oliver's stupidity, then set off at a trot, his walking stick rapping sharply against the rocky ground.

"Hey!" Oliver raced to catch up. "I came here to rescue you! Me and the kite—"

Great-uncle Gilbert whirled about and seized Oliver by the shoulders. "My kite!" he shouted. "Of course! My brave kite! Where is it?"

"Let go!" yelped Oliver, struggling. Great-uncle Gilbert was as deceptively strong as ever. Oliver thrust the kite into his great-uncle's face. "It's right here! See?"

Great-uncle Gilbert waved his hand dismissively. "That's not my kite. My kite is one of the most beautiful creations that has ever come from human hands. It is a soaring masterwork."

It was true that the kite was worse for wear. It might have been shot from the same cannon as Oliver. "Well, this is it," Oliver said. "It's been through a lot. All to rescue you, I might add."

Great-uncle Gilbert's eyebrows arched upward. He bent down to examine the kite. For a moment, he was perfectly still.

"My kite!" he finally screeched. "My poor kite! What has he done to you?" He snatched the kite from Oliver. "He broke you, didn't he! How dare he!"

"I didn't break it!" said Oliver, hurt.

Great-uncle Gilbert shook his head. "Not you. *Him!* The evil me!"

"I'm sorry," said Oliver, trying to keep his voice from trembling. "I tried to stop him."

"I'm sure you did," Great-uncle Gilbert said, patting Oliver absently on the shoulder. "But what could you have done? Even I was fooled at first! And if he fooled *me,* then what chance could *you* have possibly had?"

"Hey," said Oliver crossly, "I—"

But Great-uncle Gilbert was trotting away, muttering "Tried to warn him . . . did my best to keep him safe . . . and do I get a word of thanks?" His feet sent up clouds of dust that swirled away in the breeze.

Oliver rushed after him. He could barely keep up with the old man as he strode rapidly along, twisting and turning expertly through the desert scrub. "Can you fix the kite?" he asked anxiously.

"Can I fix the kite?" Great-uncle Gilbert replied haughtily. "My dear boy! My kitesmithing skills are unparalleled! I—"

"Well, can you?" interrupted Oliver.

"No."

Great-uncle Gilbert halted suddenly. He held the kite close to his face. His expert fingers danced, tenderly, across every inch of silk. When he came to Two's makeshift spine, he snarled, "Amateur!"

Oliver felt unexpectedly defensive. "He didn't have much time!"

"Time?" said Great-uncle Gilbert. "Time is just a construct!"

"What?"

"Never mind." The old man set off again. "I can't fix the kite."

"But why not?" panted Oliver, jogging after him.

The old man sighed. "Insufficient materials!"

"But what about the riven oak?" said Oliver. "It must have an equivalent in this world. You could use bits from it to fix the kite!"

His great-uncle stopped short. "Why, yes," he said, surprised. "How do you know about that?"

"Oh, I've learned a thing or two the last few days," said Oliver smugly.

"Perhaps you have," Great-uncle Gilbert said. "Yes, in my talented hands, the kite can be repaired with a spar from its home oak. But you see, wonderful as these trees are, they are too small to fashion spars of suitable length." He started off again in a swirl of purple robe, leaving Oliver in a cloud of dust.

Coughing, Oliver reached for his pack. "Wait!" he shouted. Oliver removed one of the branches he had collected in the last Windblowne and caught up to his great-uncle. The kite began to shake in his great-uncle's grasp. The old man jolted to a stop, gaping at the kite. Oliver stuck the branch in his face. "Here!"

Great-uncle Gilbert's eyes widened, then narrowed, then widened. "Astonishing!" he cried. He tossed his walking stick to the ground and yanked the branch out of Oliver's hands. He sniffed it all along its length. He gave it a shake. Finally he snorted and looked away.

"Well?" asked Oliver.

"Remarkable," said Great-uncle Gilbert with a sniff. "Never have I seen such a potent specimen of oak." This admission seemed pulled from him with great difficulty.

"I have more," said Oliver. "I got them from a world where the oaks were twice as high—"

But the old man was in motion again. The branch had disappeared somewhere within his robes, and he and his walking stick were barreling through the desert.

Oliver caught up and panted alongside his great-uncle. Great-uncle Gilbert seemed to know exactly where he was going, but Oliver felt as lost as he had when he landed on the world with only one moon. He turned around and around until the twisted little oaks snapped into place like the majestic trees of the other Windblownes. It wasn't easy, but soon he had a map of his own Windblowne. He knew where they were and where they were heading—to his great-uncle's oak, or rather, the oak that held his treehouse in the other Windblownes.

"So you've got the branches. Now you can fix the kite, right?"

"Only partly," huffed Great-uncle Gilbert. His voice did not sound quite so rude. "Nothing can be done about the rips in its sails. I have no silk."

"Wait," said Oliver. This time his great-uncle waited. Oliver rummaged again. He produced the silken half-tail that Ilia had given him. He had promised Ilia that he would give it to her Oliver, but this was a special situation.

Great-uncle Gilbert accepted the tail without snatching or yanking. He appraised it carefully. He coughed and puffed for a minute, then patted Oliver on the head. "Well done," he said, and the tail went away somewhere in his robes, too.

"So—you can fix the kite?" Oliver demanded for the third time.

"Possibly," said Great-uncle Gilbert, taking off again. "There is a sickness that infects these samples." He twirled a finger in his hair. "Still, there *may* be a way around that problem."

Oliver had the impression that his great-uncle had not fully considered the implications of repairing the kite. The old man had the mildest expression on his face, as though he were simply enjoying a midsummer dash. Meanwhile, a thousand miles of howling hell-world loomed emptily in all directions. Oliver reminded himself that his great-uncle was mad.

Gently, he said, "So Lord Gilbert trapped you here. But we can escape once the kite is fixed."

Oliver seemed to have earned a little grudging respect, for his great-uncle answered in a way that suggested normal conversation.

"Unfortunately for you," he said with a smile as they wound their way across the rocky slope, "even if I can repair my dear little kite, it will not be able to fly you out. The night winds on this world are not strong enough. There's no leaving here!"

Not only did Great-uncle Gilbert not seem upset about the prospect of being trapped in the hell-world, he seemed oddly cheerful about it. Oliver started to feel less gentle and more irate. "Aren't you worried about spending the rest of your life imprisoned in a hell-world?"

Great-uncle Gilbert cackled. "A hell-world? I suppose that old fool did see it that way. But my dear boy, I am not imprisoned. I like it here!"

Oliver looked around. He saw desert landscape, endless sand, and distant dust devils roaring across the parched landscape. "How could you like it? Don't you miss the oaks?"

"Miss them?" cried Great-uncle Gilbert. "Why ever would I! They're all around!" He waved his hand vaguely around his head.

"Yes, but . . . look at them. They're stunted. They're not really oaks at all."

Great-uncle Gilbert chuckled. "They're not? Lad, these are the finest oaks I have ever seen! Look closer!"

Oliver sidled over skeptically and peered at the nearest little tree. He looked at the wide-spreading branches, tough bark, and roots snaking out in all directions. He looked at the spiny little protrusions—you could hardly call them leaves—and realized with surprise that these oaks still had them. After the surge that had wiped out the leaves in the last Windblowne, he'd thought every oak in all the worlds must be entirely bare. Yet here they were. Oliver tugged on a spiky leaf. It refused to come off. He looked closer. This leaf was tiny and hard to read, like the script in an ancient book, but he could see that, in another world, this was a sentinel oak.

Oliver looked at the dry sand and cracked rock from which the oaks grew. He looked up at the cloudless orange sky. These snaking roots must grow that way in order to seek out water wherever it could be found. He stroked his hand along the oak's tough bark. This hard skin would be needed to hold in the little water the roots collected. And the tree's small size was the most efficient way to grow in desert conditions. The tenacious oaks had found a way to survive in a harsh and unforgiving environment.

"I see," said Oliver simply.

Great-uncle Gilbert beamed. "Well done, then."

"One of our world's oaks couldn't survive here at all, could it?" said Oliver. "These oaks really are stronger."

"Indeed," replied his great-uncle. "You know, Oliver, at first I assumed you were as impossibly stupid as the rest of them, but now I see that I was not completely right!"

Oliver decided to take that as a compliment. "The rest of them?"

"Yes! The rest of the fools in Windblowne! I told them of the old legends—that the oaks of our mountain are linked with oaks in the others, and that the night winds blow across them all—but they wouldn't listen. Banned me from the Festival. Fools! It's really that they didn't like losing every year, you know. It was all pure professional jealousy!"

Oliver sensed that Great-uncle Gilbert was headed off into another rant. "How many worlds are there, anyway?" he asked, trying to divert him.

Great-uncle Gilbert shook his head. "I don't know. Thousands. Millions. Billions!"

"Then I got really lucky," said Oliver, "finding you among all of them."

Great-uncle Gilbert gave him a blank stare. "Lucky? No, I'd call it exceedingly clever of you to have realized that I designed that handvane to guide me home."

"Oh . . . yes," said Oliver. "Clever of me. Exceedingly." He looked doubtfully at the desert expanse. Though it didn't seem as barren and dead as it had before, it was definitely not home.

"Actually," he went on after a thoughtful pause, "it was really Ilia who—"

"Never got a chance to try it out myself, of course," his great-uncle interrupted. "Can't take off with the kite. Too fat!" He patted his enormous stomach happily. "Appreciate your testing it out for me, lad. You do have your uses!"

"Any time," replied Oliver.

A chill breeze rose, and Oliver shivered. Though his great-uncle might like it here, he was nevertheless a prisoner of Lord Gilbert. And the hunters were doubtless on their way.

If Great-uncle Gilbert was worried about that, he certainly didn't show it. He pushed on, busily pointing out various features of the landscape. There was a hidden spring that sent a stream of clear water trickling over the rocks, and strange prickly bushes with edible fruit. "Delicious roots, too," said Great-uncle Gilbert.

Oliver could not imagine eating a root, but he supposed he would have to get used to it. Or at least he would have, if the clock were not ticking toward doom for thousands, millions, or billions of worlds. He made several attempts to point out the danger.

"So, you see," he said after describing the world of

giant oaks, "the entire forest lost its leaves at once. Lord Gilbert has activated the rest of the hunters. He—"

"Look!" cried Great-uncle Gilbert. "A snake! Marvelous!" He attempted to chase after it, but the startled snake slithered off in a blink.

Oliver sighed and followed his great-uncle. Soon they burst into a small clearing.

"Home," announced Great-uncle Gilbert with an imperial sweep of his hand.

Oliver stared, amazed. His great-uncle had built the beginnings of a new treehouse. Not a house up in the tree, because these oaks were too small for that, but a small hut with a low roof formed from the spreading branches of a little oak. Walls were constructed with branches bound together. Large rocks served as furniture. Great-uncle Gilbert hadn't wasted any time.

"You've made a house!" said Oliver, surprised.

"Brilliantly observed," said Great-uncle Gilbert. "What else would I do? Got to live in something!"

"But don't you want to go back home to Windblowne?" asked Oliver.

Great-uncle Gilbert snorted and sprawled on a

couchlike rock. "Why would I? I've got my privacy at last! Delightful. If only I could find some chickens, life would be perfect!"

"What do you mean? You had plenty of privacy in Windblowne!"

But his great-uncle was staring into space, muttering, "Chickens . . . chickens . . . where to find some chickens?"

Home, thought Oliver. Great-uncle Gilbert's handvane had known all along. The crazy old man had set up shop in the hell-world without thinking twice.

Oliver grabbed his great-uncle's arm and shook it. This was no time for the old man's eccentricities. "Great-uncle Gilbert!"

"Eh, what? Oliver!" His great-uncle seemed newly startled by Oliver's presence. Oliver repeated his question.

"Privacy in Windblowne? Hardly! Too many presumptuous boys prowling around, zapping me off to other worlds!"

"You mean Two, right?" said Oliver.

Great-uncle Gilbert waved his hand airily. "Is that what you call him? Yes. Atrociously behaved. No surprise, considering the appalling savagery of his caretaker!" He leapt up and darted about, searching for something. "At first the boy wanted to know about kites. Admirable! Happy to oblige such a talented lad, of course—"

Oliver winced.

"—but they couldn't fool me for long! Not with a barrage of letters from *him,* demanding to know all my secrets! The old fool wanted to control the paths between worlds for his own ends and was willing to employ the most brutal means to do it. You must have seen those black strings—"

"Wires," corrected Oliver importantly.

"Strings everywhere, sucking life from the oaks!" cried Great-uncle Gilbert. "And the old madman wanted *me* to work for *him*! Can you imagine that?" He broke into an insane giggle. Then his eyes widened, and he thrust a hand into his robe. His face brightened, and he pulled a carving knife from a pocket. "There you are!" he said, wagging a finger at the knife. "Hiding in my pocket all along. Now, let's have a look at the oak."

Oliver's heart fell when he saw the riven oak. The little tree was nearly dead. Most of its spiny leaves had fallen, and its branches drooped against the ground.

Oliver knelt beside it and stroked the withered branches. Though afraid of what he would see, he turned to look at the kite, hoping there was enough strength left in the oak to—

Yes. The kite fluttered slightly in Great-uncle Gilbert's hands. But the master kitesmith was frowning.

"Can you fix it?" Oliver said.

"Stop asking me that," said his great-uncle. "I can fix it." But he sounded a little unsure, and his eyes were glistening with tears.

"It's a terrible thing," Great-uncle Gilbert said sadly, "and it's all my fault. That madman would never have known about the Way Between Worlds if it hadn't been for me."

"No," said Oliver, "he would have figured it out. You all seem to have a knack for that." And he told Great-uncle Gilbert about Ilia's Windblowne, where an Oliver had been carried away by one of his great-uncle's kites.

For once, Great-uncle Gilbert listened intently, dabbing at his eyes with one sleeve.

"Fascinating," he said when Oliver had finished. "There is more to this than even I knew. You must tell me everything about your adventures. Come, I'll work on the kite.

But first, we'll need just a bit of this." He leaned over with his carving knife and cut a branch from the riven oak. "It will have to be enough," he said, looking at it doubtfully.

"Why do you need that?" asked Oliver.

"Do not question—"began Great-uncle Gilbert, then stopped. He started again, gently. "The oaks in this world, as you have noticed, have special qualities. It will help if I can use a bit of one of them in the kite."

They trudged solemnly over to the house-in-progress. Oliver sat on one of the chair-rocks while Great-uncle Gilbert spread the kite out on the ground. His fingers searched the kite, testing, probing. "Fine work by that boy, fine work," he mused. "Surprising how close he came, really." From deep within his robe he pulled tools, twine, and a mix of other objects. The branches and tail that Oliver had brought were also produced, and then Great-uncle Gilbert's hands began to dart about so quickly that Oliver could scarcely tell what was happening.

"This other you is really quite talented," Great-uncle Gilbert said after a minute. "You must be immensely jealous!"

"You don't have to put it like that," said Oliver, hurt.

But then he realized he wasn't jealous. He felt proud of Two, and of himself. After all, he was the one who had brought the crimson kite back to Great-uncle Gilbert. He wasn't sure that Two could have done that. He informed Great-uncle Gilbert of this.

"Of course, of course!" said his great-uncle, slapping his knee. "Outstanding work, lad. Especially considering *he* managed to dispose of *me* so easily. Not an easy task, I assure you."

This had been bothering Oliver for some time. "That was my fault," he admitted. "You could have fought off the hunters if I hadn't distracted you."

"Not at all, my boy!" announced Great-uncle Gilbert heartily. "My fault entirely. I shouldn't have sent you away. I should have told you everything, brought you into my confidence. You could have been of great help to me! Now tell me all that has happened to you. I want to hear everything."

Now we're getting somewhere, thought Oliver. He told Great-uncle Gilbert the entire tale, from the kite's arrival at his window to his discovery of Lord Gilbert's Windblowne. He told of his escape and his quest to find and rescue his great-uncle. (Oliver thought he detected a glistening tear during that part of the story, which Great-uncle Gilbert tried to hide by draping a piece of silk over his head.) He told of his adventures across the other Windblownes and how he had learned to leap with the night winds. During it all, Great-uncle Gilbert worked on the kite with ferocious intensity, reaching into the recesses of his robe and finding silken thread, needles, packets of paste, more knives, and handfuls of chicken feed.

"Amazing!" said Great-uncle Gilbert. "Remarkable! To think you are able to use the oaks as a map to get around the mountain. And to identify the precise oak from which a leaf has fallen! All of that requires powers of observation even keener than my own."

"Does it?" said Oliver, puzzled. "I thought everyone could do that."

"Everyone can't," said Great-uncle Gilbert firmly. "You notice things, lad. You know how to pay attention to the world. A very valuable talent. Now——" He held up the kite, which was looking much better.

"It's still not moving," Oliver said.

"Not to worry." Great-uncle Gilbert slipped the spine from its braces. "The boy almost had it. Almost. But it requires the touch of a master!" He seized the branch he had taken from the desert oak and clipped a bit from one end. Then he flourished his carving knife and went to work, the knife glinting in the sun. Within moments, he was done. Carefully, he slid the modified spine into place. It fit perfectly.

"There," said Great-uncle Gilbert. "That should do—"

But before he could finish, the crimson kite leapt from his hands and shot into the air. Oliver whooped and cheered as the kite turned delighted loops. Then, with a sudden swoop, the kite flew down and settled in Oliver's hands, fluttering its sails happily.

"Well, there's gratitude for you," Great-uncle Gilbert said petulantly, but he had a smug smile.

Oliver grinned. "It's good to have you back," he said to the kite, and with a whirl he sent it flying, its long tail swirling behind it.

"Not just back," said Great-uncle Gilbert, swelling with self-satisfaction, "but better than ever. The kite is now composed of materials from four worlds and has been given the strengths of each. The verdant potency of one world! The stubborn persistence of another! Truly extraordinary."

Oliver took the old spine. "Now we have to destroy this," he said. "The hunters are using it to track the kite."

"Very forward-thinking of you, lad," mused his great-uncle. "We'll put it in the fire on which I'll cook our lunch."

For lunch they feasted on a kind of watery soup made from Great-uncle Gilbert's stores of roots and berries. Oliver didn't think he had ever enjoyed a meal more. They watched the kite fly high overhead, exploring the sky. Oliver wished he could fly with it. Great-uncle Gilbert said the night winds would not be strong enough for that, but Oliver was determined to give it a try anyway.

"I have to find a way off this world," he said. "We've bought ourselves a little time, but it won't take Lord Gilbert long to figure out that I've destroyed the spar they were tracking, which means the kite is fixed, which means I've found you. He's sure to send the hunters here."

"Agreed," said Great-uncle Gilbert. "We need a defense."

"How can you defend against anything?" Oliver asked. "You didn't get here by kite. Lord Gilbert can pull you back through the machine anytime he wants."

Great-uncle Gilbert smiled and patted Oliver on the head. "I learned much from that first encounter." He shrugged aside his robe to reveal a latticework of short desert-oak branches, woven together in a kind of armor over his shirt. He tapped one of them. "Fool me once, not twice! This will disrupt his infernal signals. He won't take me so easily this time. And I know enough now to fend off those three hunters!"

Oliver shook his head. "Sixty-two hunters, at least, and maybe more." He described the massive leaf-death on the world with one moon.

"Sixty-two, eh?" Great-uncle Gilbert looked concerned. "Then I—that is, we—had best get started."

For the rest of the day, Great-uncle Gilbert worked on his defense, and Oliver helped him, or at least tried to. His great-uncle believed the hunters could be fought using a system of nets and catapults, which he had constructed from available materials. Oliver rather doubted this. He tried to help anyway, but never having been handy with tools, he kept making mistakes. He had the impression that his great-uncle thought he was getting in the way more than helping, but at least he was being nicer about it. While they worked, Great-uncle Gilbert babbled on in the most interesting way about the history of Windblowne, its old legends, stories that Oliver had never heard. For example, his great-uncle claimed that many centuries ago, before there had been a Windblowne in the trees, people had lived in a system of caves under the mountain.

"Where are the caves now?" asked Oliver.

Great-uncle Gilbert shook his head. "Don't know. I've never been able to find them."

Oliver was impressed. Windblownians had always considered themselves to be the first people on the mountain. Oliver gathered that the ancient book he had seen in Great-uncle Gilbert's treehouse came from the age before there was a town on the mountain, and that his great-uncle considered it very precious. "My books are the one thing I truly miss," he told Oliver wistfully.

"Even my father's books?" Oliver asked.

"Ah yes, your father's histories! A bit long-winded but fascinating all the same. His description of old Windblownian legends launched my own research."

"What about your kites?" asked Oliver. "Don't you miss them, too?"

"Yes. But I can make new kites. I have ideas for

miniature kites, which can be made from these oaks. The books, however—there is far more to these worlds than it seems, and those ancient texts are the key. The books are irreplaceable." He sighed heavily.

For supper Oliver shared the last of the sandwiches he had gotten from Ilia, and they drank the clear water of the spring. At sunset, their work on the defensive measures complete, Oliver and Great-uncle Gilbert sat comfortably as the winds sighed over them. Under the light of the two moons, they looked out over the vast black desert, the winds bringing smells from the other side of this world and, Oliver suspected, from other worlds as well.

Soon he decided the time had come to test the kite. Seeming to sense what he wanted, the kite flew to him, and he made excuses to his great-uncle, who sat quietly, staring into the vastness.

Oliver picked his way to the crest under a sky full of stars. Distant mountains made jagged silhouettes on the horizon. The night winds whistled gently. "Ready?" he said to the kite. It responded with a determined shake. Oliver launched it into the sky.

Though the kite did its best, tugging at Oliver from

every angle, there was not nearly enough wind to lift them both. Oliver even tried a few running jumps, but it did no good. He wasn't going anywhere.

The kite flew near him, sails drooping in shame. "It's not your fault," Oliver protested. "There just isn't enough wind." But the kite drifted away, low to the ground, back toward the house.

Great. Now everyone's depressed. Oliver crouched on the crest, thinking furiously. There had to be something he could do.

All around him blew the whispery winds of the desert night.

Your talents lie elsewhere, Great-uncle Gilbert had said to him, in a time that seemed long ago.

Oliver closed his eyes, listening, paying attention to the world. The winds' touch was featherlight and cold. It was the only thing he could hear. There were no bird-calls, no sounds of animals hunting, nothing rising up from the mountain below.

If you do whisper, O winds, then whisper to me, of oaks which dwell across the worlds.

They came again, the words Great-uncle Gilbert had scrawled in his precious book. A book written during a time when, perhaps, the oaks had whispered. *Maybe that's what the whispers were,* Oliver thought. The sound of the night winds blowing through the oaks, across all the worlds.

Oliver remembered how the wind had sounded in each of the worlds he had seen. He thought of the lush forest of the last world. The howling winds there had been the most powerful that he had ever heard, as they coursed through the branches of the immense, ancient oaks.

He imagined that he could hear them now.

He held his breath and listened.

It wasn't his imagination. He *could* hear them.

They were there, far away, deep under the sound of the whispering desert winds, like a river running underneath the world.

Oliver rose to his feet and reached out. They seemed to draw him onward.

He took a step.

Darkness enclosed him, and there was a sudden vertiginous lurch as he balanced on the edge of a void that fell away forever on all sides. He ran forward, eyes closed, clinging to the sound of the night winds from the potent world of one moon.

And then a windburst hit, his breath exploded from him, and he opened his eyes. Above him glowed Aspin, alone. Under his feet lay thick, springy grass. He screamed and fell backward. He landed not on grass but on the rocky ground of the desert crest.

His heart hammered. What had just happened? Had he imagined it?

No, he thought in wonder. He held up one hand, felt the gentle breeze play across his fingers. These were the winds that blew across worlds.

He had to tell Great-uncle Gilbert.

FLASH

FLASH

FLASH

Oliver whipped around. The light from the flashes was already dying, but he could see three black shapes flying against the backdrop of stars.

Three more flashes came, then three more.

Oliver began to run.

The flashes came regularly as Oliver raced toward Great-uncle Gilbert's new treehouse. In the distance he could see nets going up one after another. Captured hunters were plummeting toward the ground while others flew around them, slashing at the nets with their metal talons. Most of the hunters were freed before they hit the ground. The crimson kite seemed to be everywhere at once, leading hunters into the nets, always one twist ahead of the grasping claws.

Oliver staggered and slid through the sand, shouting, trying to distract the hunters. But they seemed to have no interest in anything other than the kite and Great-uncle Gilbert, who had to be running out of nets. More hunters were flashing in every few seconds.

Oliver reached the treehouse. Great-uncle Gilbert was struggling with a new net, his eyes wide and fierce. "Oliver!" he shouted. "Get that side!"

Oliver grasped the other end of the net.

But the hunters had broken through. One struck at Great-uncle Gilbert's right arm, talons gripping. Three more landed on his left arm. The hunters shrieked, and to Oliver they had never sounded more like shrieks of pain. The old man flung aside his robe, momentarily freeing himself, but several more hunters attacked, grasping his shirt and oaken armor.

The crimson kite dove, five hunters just behind. Its long

tail whipped out and lashed around Great-uncle Gilbert's waist. The kite heaved, trying to pull the old man free—

FLASH

but there was a blinding glare as all the hunters flashed away at once. Great-uncle Gilbert and the crimson kite were gone.

Triumphant shrieks came from everywhere. A host of flashes turned night into day, and then the fleet of hunters disappeared.

Only one hunter remained. It circled above Oliver in complete silence. It looked at him with its cold glass eyes, then turned and flew lazily skyward. With a last bright flash, it vanished.

Oliver lowered the net. The hunter had not even bothered with him.

The crimson kite was what Lord Gilbert wanted, and now he had it. He wanted Great-uncle Gilbert, too. But he didn't want Oliver any longer, and so he had abandoned him in what Lord Gilbert considered to be the hell-world.

But I know something that no one else does. Oliver raced back to the peak.

At first he could hear nothing but the desert wind and the blood pounding in his ears. *Calm down,* he told himself.

He closed his eyes and listened for the night winds.

He listened to the desert wind, blowing across endless miles to the crest.

Then under it came a deeper sound, rich and full. Whispering through the oaks across all the worlds.

This time he heard another sound within it, a keening cry of pain. A dying voice, a voice that he had heard again and again in one world after another, a voice that had once called to him so strongly that its cry pierced his head like a knife.

The riven oak.

The terrible headache returned, the pain making it almost impossible to listen. He concentrated on the winds, searching through each of them. He heard the hollow howl of winds trapped inside the Crest Wall. He heard again the shout of the winds of the world with one moon.

Then he found what he was searching for. The voice of the winds that he had heard each night of his life. The voice of the winds outside his bedroom window.

He turned to them, and they grew louder. He reached for them, and they blew straight to him.

He did not open his eyes. It was easier to track the voice if he was not distracted. And so he felt rather than saw the limitless darkness around him, felt a thousand, a million, a billion different winds whipping around him, each carrying a cry of confusion and fear. Oliver let them rush past, realizing that if his attention wandered to any of them, he could lose the voice he was following through the void.

He stepped forward, into the winds.

20

Home, thought Oliver as he ran, throwing himself fearlessly through the night winds, allowing them to hurl him in exhilarating leaps down the crest. He needed their speed—if he wasn't fast, if his final plan did not work, then it was entirely possible that he was seeing his Windblowne for the very last time.

They went on with the Festival, he thought as he raced through the night. Every oak in Windblowne had the aspect of midwinter, entirely bereft of leaves. Oliver wondered how the townspeople could go on as normal with signs of disaster looming all around them. But go on they had. Just inside the oakline, safe from the night winds, viewing stands were tarped over and strapped securely to the ground. Debris from the Festival—posters, score sheets, tournament results—whipped through the air along with a thick whirl of oak leaves.

Oliver ran through his world, the familiar winds murmuring around him, thinking of his kite, his great-uncle, and so many other beings in so many Windblownes who were all depending on the success of his final plan.

When he returned to the oakline he was panting and sweating and carrying a bulky bundle wrapped in a large blanket.

Leaving Windblowne this second time was very hard. "Goodbye," he said, just in case.

He leapt up the crest, listening for the painful sound of the night winds blowing through the oaks on Lord Gilbert's world. At first he feared he would not be able to find the subtle voices again.

No, he told himself. *Pay attention to the world. Listen.*

The anxious thoughts and fears slid away. Somewhere beneath the desperate urgency, Oliver listened.

And then came that keening wail of pain, the heartbreaking cry of the riven oak.

He closed his eyes as the other winds quieted.

He found the wind that led to that voice and strode confidently toward it.

He walked between worlds.

And then he was standing on the crest again. Not his home crest, he knew before he opened his eyes, but Lord Gilbert's. He could feel the difference in the ground beneath him, smell it in the air around him, and hear it in the deep raging rumble of the winds. He could feel it in the terrible pain of the headache returning, as the winds blew through the riven oak. He pushed it softly away, and the headache faded.

He opened his eyes.

The night was burning.

Down the mountain, Lord Gilbert's treehouse blazed like a torch, sending a beam of light into the night sky. The spiderweb network of wires blazed too, buzzing and crackling, draining the oaks in this world and all the others, focusing everything into Lord Gilbert's machines. Sparks danced along the wires in circles around the oakline, surrounding the crest in a cage of lightning. The cage affected even the night winds, for as the lightning brightened, the winds diminished to a stiff gale.

He looked to the sky, hoping. His heart leapt as he saw that the crimson kite had not been captured. Seven hunters pursued the kite as it fought and dodged valiantly.

In fives and sixes, more hunters were rising to help the others. A buzzing sound from the wires filled the air. The hunters shrieked in pain. With the treehouse shining and the wires blazing, it was as though night had been eliminated; the stars were washed out by the glare.

Oliver realized that, after all his travels, he had found the hell-world at last.

And he had only seconds before the hunters spotted him. Now that Oliver had escaped his banishment, Lord Gilbert would surely order the hunters to attack.

He crouched and began unwrapping the bundle frantically, wishing he had not been forced to wrap it so securely, wondering what had made him think this mad plan would ever work—

"Oliver!"

Two was limping across the oakline underneath the lightning storm, the treehouse beam behind him casting a long shadow up the crest. Two tossed his green-and-black power kite upward into the gale and flew toward the peak. Oliver took in the other boy's terrified face. He looked, if possible, worse than he had the last time Oliver had seen him. His hair had thinned, he'd lost more weight, and—

Two reached him, stumbled, and fell, gasping. His voice shook with fear and fury.

"I knew you'd be here. . . . He's activated them all. . . . He has your great-uncle. . . . You have to get away. . . ."

Above them, sheer numbers had overwhelmed the crimson kite. Eight hunters had grasped it in their talons, yet still it fought, dragging them all across the sky. The rest of the hunters—dozens now—had spotted Oliver and were veering toward him.

Oliver calmly untied the final knot. "Get behind me," he ordered Two.

"But you have to—"

"NOW!" shouted Oliver, rising.

Two crawled behind Oliver. "But there's no way to stop the hunters," he said, quaking.

"Yes," said Oliver, "there is."

The cloud of hunters wheeled and dove, shrieking.

Oliver threw open his bundle.

The kite-eater burst free from the blanket and shot into the sky.

The hunters veered, but it was too late. The kite-eater smashed into them, gnashing and twisting, exploding the cloud in a dozen different directions.

"The kite-eater!" shouted Two, stunned. "But—"

"Kites," said Oliver, watching with arms folded as a pitched battle commenced in the skies overhead. One of his plans had worked, finally, exactly as he'd intended. "The hunters are just another kind of kite."

"Yes," coughed Two. "But won't it eat the crimson kite?"

"No," answered Oliver impatiently. The kite-eater was hurtling straight at the captive kite and the hunters holding it. Four of them broke away to face the new threat. "I told it I was going to rescue Great-uncle Gilbert, and that it better obey me if it wanted to save him."

With deadly twists and sharp bites, the kite-eater chased off its foes and resumed its charge. The last four hunters were flying erratically now, as the crimson kite thrashed fiercely. With the kite-eater nearly on them, the hunters released the kite with furious shrieks and hurtled away, barely escaping the kite-eater's snapping jaws.

The two kites circled each other warily. But the kite-eater had clearly taken Oliver's orders seriously, and it turned to chase after a nearby hunter.

Oliver reached up, and from high above, his crimson kite dropped and settled into his grasp.

"Good kite," said Oliver proudly. The kite fluttered its sails defiantly.

The Olivers watched as the hunters scattered all around the sky, pursued by the speedy kite-eater.

"It's not going to hurt the hunters, is it?" asked Two anxiously.

"No," said Oliver. He gave a piercing whistle, and high overhead the kite-eater paused. For a moment, Oliver feared that the kite-eater would not obey, but then it broke off its pursuit of the hunters and began flying broad, protective circles around the Olivers. The hunters flew back and forth in the distance, screeching, but came no closer.

"It listened to you!" said Two.

"I wasn't sure that it would," Oliver admitted.

Two tried to rise but fell back into a sitting position. Oliver looked at him, worried. "Are you going to be all right?"

Two shook his head. "Don't worry about me. You have to take the kite and get out of here right now. Lord Gilbert has all kinds of machines and secret weapons you haven't even seen yet. He can't be stopped."

Oliver stroked his kite, which fluttered firmly in response. "I have secret weapons now, too."

He heard the winds blowing from the riven oak, a painful cry, but he knew he could not go to the oak, not yet. He had to stay on the crest, where he and the winds were strongest. He knew Lord Gilbert would come for them.

Lord Gilbert did not disappoint.

Down the mountain, the pillar of light brightened. The buzzing in the air—and the cry of pain in Oliver's head—grew louder. Oliver could see sparks jumping along the wires.

"What's he doing?" Oliver asked, beginning to worry. Despite what he had told Two, he had not counted on any secret weapons.

"It's the disc," said Two miserably, sinking again to his knees. "It . . ."

A dark blotch appeared in the pillar of light, rising from the oaktops. Oliver could see a silhouette growing larger—a man, perched on the mirror-like disc. The disc was rising smoothly along the metal shaft, and Lord Gilbert was riding it to the top.

The disc reached the very top of the shaft, and with hardly a pause, it detached and rose into the air.

Oliver gasped. The disc could fly.

Bolts of lightning flashed from the bottom of the disc

as it drifted toward the crest, carrying Lord Gilbert majestically.

Oliver took a step back. He had not expected anything like this.

Two moaned with fear. "It's too late," he cried.

Oliver murmured to his kite, keeping his voice low in case Lord Gilbert had some means of listening. He whispered his final plan, and the kite twisted urgently, quivering but resolute. Oliver felt a surge of love for the kite. He hoped they both survived the next few seconds.

The disc approached. Bursts of lightning from beneath the disc stabbed through the darkness, leaping from the platform to the wires. Lord Gilbert, on the platform, continued wobbling toward the crest, his fingers dancing on the HM IV. The tower of light from the treehouse threw everything into weird, broken shadows, and the winds screamed as they blasted against the crackling cage of lightning. The sounds should have stifled anything Lord Gilbert had to say, but his voice was amplified like thunder:

"OLIVER! RETURN TO YOUR MASTER!"

"Oliver One or Oliver Two?" shouted Oliver.

The voice made a sound of strangled rage. "BOTH OF YOU! OBEY ME AT ONCE, OR—"

Two broke from behind Oliver, running toward Lord Gilbert. The disc was hovering just above the ground now, thirty feet away from them.

"No!" shouted Oliver. "Don't!"

Two made a hideous sound, unleashing years of misery and pain and humiliation into a single cry. He brandished a thick spar, whittled to a point. Oliver had not seen him take it from beneath his jacket.

Lord Gilbert laughed, and his hand twitched on the HM IV. Two froze, then fell, his arm still raised in defiance.

Oliver could only watch helplessly. If he got too close to Lord Gilbert, the HM IV would paralyze him, too.

"You ruined my plumbing!" screeched Lord Gilbert, pointing at Oliver.

"Why don't you come and get me, then?" Oliver could see that the disc was having trouble with the gale. It bucked and swayed, requiring Lord Gilbert to continually adjust course with the HM IV.

"Having trouble?" Oliver taunted.

Lord Gilbert spat and made more motions on the HM IV. The disc made a strained hum as it fought its way uphill. Oliver felt a numbness creeping up his legs.

Oliver wobbled on the grass as he watched Lord Gilbert

draw near. The winds coiled around him. The crimson kite held its sails wide open, gathering wind, ready.

Oliver could no longer feel his feet. He sagged to his knees.

"Go!" he shouted, and released the crimson kite.

The kite streaked toward Lord Gilbert, fast as the winds. As Oliver tipped over, now completely paralyzed, he saw Lord Gilbert raise an arm to protect himself—the arm that wore the HM IV. The kite smashed into the device at blinding speed. Lord Gilbert screamed, and the HM IV went tumbling down the mountain, sparking and bouncing. A crimson blur—the kite—went hurtling in another direction.

And the numbness was gone.

The cloud of hunters dispersed instantly, their cries fading into the distance.

Two rose shakily to his feet.

Oliver pushed himself onto his hands and saw Lord Gilbert jump free of the out-of-control platform, which crashed away at the mercy of the winds.

Then Lord Gilbert was stumbling after the HM IV.

The crimson blur came by. Oliver grasped the tail of his kite. They covered the distance to Lord Gilbert in a second. Oliver released the kite's tail, and with the winds at his back, he leapt onto the old man, grabbing his arm.

"You're coming with me," said Oliver. He closed his eyes and stepped into the winds.

Oliver found that the journey from one world to the next was considerably more difficult when dragging a spitting, screeching, struggling great-uncle by one arm. He could feel Lord Gilbert's thin wrist beneath his fingers, and he could feel a hand clawing at him, but he pretended those things were a thousand miles away. New worlds called to him from all directions, and Oliver told them, *Someday, someday* . . .

Then he was stepping onto rocky ground, the soft murmur of the desolate desert winds all around him.

Lord Gilbert screamed, and Oliver released him in distaste.

The old man backed away, chest heaving, eyes bulging as he gazed wildly at the vast, moonslit distances of the desert mountain. "The hell-world! How did you do this?" he breathed.

Oliver shook his head. "This is not the hell-world. The hell-world is something you made for yourself."

Lord Gilbert grabbed for Oliver, but Oliver leapt aside. "Stop it!" Oliver ordered. "Stop it or I'm leaving."

Lord Gilbert's eyes narrowed, but he came no closer. "You're going to leave me here anyway, aren't you? You intend this world to become my prison."

"Whether it becomes your prison or not is up to you," said Oliver.

"You can't abandon me here," snarled Lord Gilbert, stumbling backward onto a rock. "I'll die."

"No," said Oliver. "You won't die. And I'm not abandoning you." He pointed down the mountain. "You'll find a house down there. You'll see that it's been stocked with delicious roots and berries. There's a spring nearby. Follow my great-uncle's example, and you'll see that you can live well."

"No!" screamed Lord Gilbert. "I'll find a way out! I'll kill every one of these trees if I have to! I'll make them give me their secrets!"

"Harm one of these trees," said Oliver through gritted teeth, "and I will know. I'll be back here the instant it happens. And I'll take you to a world that will make this one seem like paradise."

And with that, Oliver stepped back into the winds.

21

The broken halves of the riven oak still leaned away from each other, but they were nearly touching now, held in place by an ingenious system of splints and rope.

"Be patient," Great-uncle Gilbert had told Oliver. "It will heal, but we mustn't rush it."

Oliver was astonished at the progress Great-uncle Gilbert had made in just two days. The machines and spikes and tubes were gone. The black wires had been stripped from the surrounding trees. Oliver's head still ached when he came near the riven oak, but the pain lessened each day.

In Lord Gilbert's former treehouse, Great-uncle Gilbert was still behaving as he had ever since Oliver had freed him. He was gleefully running about, maniacally pushing buttons and throwing switches. The place was in chaos as a result, and he had managed to blow up part of the kitchen. He couldn't have been happier.

"Great-uncle Gilbert," said Oliver, "I'm going home now."

"Yes, yes," said Great-uncle Gilbert. "You'll be back with my chickens, won't you?" He waved his arm in Oliver's general direction but did not look up from the laboratory table. He had the disassembled HM IV laid out before him and was poking at it with a kite spar.

Oliver rolled his eyes. "Don't worry, I'll bring the chickens. You're sure you want to stay here?"

"Of course!" cried Great-uncle Gilbert. "No distractions, no fools meddling about—er, no offense."

"None taken," said Oliver mildly.

"And," continued Great-uncle Gilbert, "I can fly my kites on the crest without that idiot mayor complaining about explosions! Without whimpering dolts whining about kites being devoured! I haven't flown a kite on the crest in forty years." He peered seriously at Oliver. "It took five Watchmen to carry me off, you know," he said.

"I know, Great-uncle Gilbert, I know," said Oliver, grinning. Some of his great-uncle's stories were becoming quite familiar.

Oliver was about to depart when Great-uncle Gilbert spoke again. "Er, Oliver . . ."

"Yes?"

Great-uncle Gilbert drummed his fingers anxiously. "It would also be . . . acceptable . . . for you to, er, visit on occasion, you know."

"I know, Great-uncle Gilbert. Don't worry, I'll visit often."

He waved goodbye as his great-uncle smiled at him from the treehouse door.

Oliver hurried to the crest as twilight neared and the shadows lengthened.

He found Two flying a kite in the crisp, fresh winds. Two was surrounded by hunters. Some of them were watching him fly his kite. Others were taking off, landing, taking off again, and chasing each other across the sky.

Two had attempted to help Oliver with his kite-flying, but after a few botched outings that seriously damaged some of Two's finest kites, Oliver had decided it just wasn't his thing. He wasn't worried about it. He had other interests now. Reaching into his pack, Oliver removed Great-uncle Gilbert's handvane—really his own handvane now, as his great-uncle had given it to him—and snapped it onto his wrist.

Two began reeling in his kite. It was a magnificent golden dragon, with tails that spun in all directions. Beside him lay a few more of his kites. Oliver had helped him pack them up the night before. There was also a suitcase full of carefully folded clothes, backpacks full of kitesmithing tools, and a portfolio of kite designs. Oliver shrugged one pack onto his shoulders, and Two gathered up everything else.

"Are you ready?" asked Oliver.

Two shifted his feet nervously and looked around the crest. "I don't know." His voice shook just slightly.

"Come on," said Oliver gently. "Everything's arranged. They can't wait to meet you. But if you don't want to go today, we can go tomorrow. There's no rush."

Two took a deep, shuddering breath. "No. I'm ready." He held out his hand. "Let's go."

Oliver took Two's hand and closed his eyes. Far off,

beneath the blustery gusts of this peak, Oliver heard the hollow roar of winds within the Crest Wall.

Two's hand gripped his arm tightly as Oliver stepped through the winds.

In a moment they stood on the crest again, this time surrounded by the wall.

Two gasped. He turned slowly, taking in the sight. "They did all of this because their Oliver was blown away on the winds?"

Oliver nodded. "And he took a few others with him."

Two looked at his folded kites. "Do you think they'll really tear it down?"

"They might," said Oliver. "I talked to the captain, and most of these Windblownians are sick of the wall. They just have to get over their fear. Maybe you can help with that."

Two was still scanning the wall. "Is that her?" he asked suddenly, pointing.

In the distance, a tiny figure was rapidly descending a rope ladder.

"Yes," said Oliver. "That's Ilia." He waved, and Ilia waved back, swinging comfortably with one hand from the rope ladder. "I'd better go."

Two turned to him, a stricken look on his face. "What if . . . what if they don't like me? Maybe we should go back."

"No," said Oliver, "this will be your Windblowne now. This will be your home."

Two took one uncertain step, then another. With each step he moved more quickly toward Ilia, who had reached the ground and was running toward him.

As Oliver stepped back into the winds, he looked toward the top of the wall, just above the rope ladder. The setting sun illuminated two familiar figures waiting there, a man and a woman huddled together, watching as Two approached Ilia.

Then Oliver stepped across worlds, back to Great-uncle Gilbert's new home.

He arrived amidst the full force of the night winds. The crimson kite was waiting. Oliver leapt and grasped its lashing tail, and they soared up into the mist.

Part of him didn't want to go home just yet. Part of him wanted to catch his first glimpse of the ocean tonight. But the part of him that was drawn toward home was stronger, and so he settled for a flight through the dark, wind-lashed Way Between Worlds, listening to the voices of the many worlds now available to him.

Morning arrived, the mist brightened, and they soared on powerful wind toward Oliver's crest. Below him, he saw an enormous crowd of people surrounding the peak, where a stage had been erected.

"The Festival awards ceremony!" Oliver said. "I completely forgot."

The kite dipped, asking if he wanted to land near the stage.

"No," said Oliver, after thinking for a moment. "Take us down near the oakline."

They shot over the crowd and the stage. Oliver saw heads turning and heard voices beginning to shout. The granite jumping marker passed beneath them, and Oliver made a clean landing at the oakline. He looked up at the powerful oaks, already putting out new green shoots on their branches, which were tossing as if in greeting. Oliver waved back to them, just in case. There were more cries from the direction of the stage, but Oliver hurried into the forest. He was too tired to deal with any of that yet.

He found Windswept Way and began the spiral walk downward. He passed a member of the Watch, bleary, plump, and old, and smiled at him. The Watchman smiled back.

"Almost back to normal!" the Watchman called to him proudly. "Another fine Festival."

Oliver found it hard to believe that the Festival had happened at all. The food stands had been taken down, the banners and flags removed, and the extra tables in front of the inns taken in. Even the posters that had littered the roads a few days ago had been swept clean, some by industrious Windblownians but most by the incessant winds.

He saw a girl bounding up the Way. It was Ilia, late for the awards, clutching a lion kite.

"Hullo, Ilia." Oliver grinned.

Ilia stopped short. "Oliver! You overslept, too? Aren't you going to the awards?"

Oliver yawned. "I don't think so. I'm really tired."

Ilia gaped, then said, "Is that your kite?"

"Yes," said Oliver proudly, realizing the kite must look strange, flying along without a line. "You should come see it fly. Meet me on the crest tonight, just before the night winds?"

Ilia stared at him as though he were mad.

"Oh, one more thing," said Oliver. He reached into a buttoned inside pocket and found a kite charm. *Ilia,* it read. He passed it to her. "Thank you," he said. "It did bring me luck."

Then he waved and headed for home.

He passed some other kids who were also racing for the crest. They aimed the usual taunts in his direction, but Oliver hardly noticed.

His treehouse, when he reached it, seemed somehow more welcoming, even though nothing about it had changed. Oliver was happy to see flickering light in his mother's blazing forge through the open doors of her workshop, and the open shutters of his father's study.

His mother came out of the workshop, dragging her newest sculpture. She must have won the battle with the mayor, for most of her sculptures stood proudly along the Way. Oliver smiled as he saw that several of them had been sold.

He went to help her.

"Oh! Hullo, dear," his mother said, surprised, as Oliver put his shoulder to the sculpture and pushed. They settled it in its appointed spot and stood back, looking it over.

This one reminded Oliver of the regal oaks of the one-moon world. He had a feeling that sometimes his mother must hear the winds whispering, too.

"I really like this one," he said.

"Really?" she replied with pleasure. "You do? You've never said that before! Thank you!" And then she swept in and gave him a fierce and proud hug.

Embarrassed, Oliver extricated himself and escaped up the treehouse steps.

His father was sitting at the kitchen table, pen scratching away. Oliver began to build a fire.

His father looked up. "Hullo, Oliver!"

"Hullo, Dad."

"It's good to see you, son. While the Festival was on, you were out at all hours, up early and back late—I don't think we saw you at all, now that I think about it!"

"Well, I *was* busy," Oliver agreed. "But it's good to see you again, too."

His father smiled and resumed writing.

"You're interested in history, aren't you?" Oliver asked.

His father dropped his pen. "Why, yes, of course! Very much!" He sighed heavily. "I'm sorry it's never interested you."

"Well," Oliver said, "I took your advice and went to see Great-uncle Gilbert."

"Who? Oh, yes," said his father. "Your mother's crazy old uncle."

"That's the one," said Oliver. "He's full of stories about Windblowne. He told me some interesting things about the mountain's history. I thought you might like to hear them."

"That would be wonderful!" Oliver's father leaned forward and pushed his journal aside. "Perhaps I could put them in another book!" Oliver had never seen his father so excited.

"Great," said Oliver, yawning. "But we'll have to talk about it tomorrow. I need some sleep. It's been a long week."

"Yes, I imagine so," said his father. "How was the Festival, anyway?"

"Oh . . . the Festival. It was fine," Oliver replied. And with a grin, he dashed upstairs to bed.

acknowledgments

Windblowne would not have been possible without the love and wisdom of my wife, Miriam Angress; the eternal patience and counsel of my fellow writers John Claude Bemis, Jennifer Harrod, and Jen Wichman; the insight of my brother-in-law, Percy Angress; my terrific agents, Josh and Tracey Adams of Adams Literary; and my magnificent editor, Jim Thomas. Much is also owed to the faith and encouragement of my readers Claudia Lanese, Indigo Sargent, and Daniel de Marchi; to the editorial assistance of Chelsea Eberly; and to my parents, Merle and Donna Messer.

about the author

Blown into this world as a baby, Stephen Messer spent his childhood flying kites on windswept hilltops in Maine and Arizona. He has lived in deserts and in megacities, on alpine mountains and in lowland swamps. Nowadays he lives with his wife in an old house surrounded by oak trees in Durham, North Carolina. Sometimes, on windblown nights, it seems as if the house has been transported to another world.